TO WIN HER LOVE

After the tragic loss of all of her family — first her brother, and then her parents — Lucy is pleased to learn she may have relatives in America. Hiram Bojangle III invites her to go and stay with him and his family on their luxury plantation in South Carolina. Hiram is keen on genealogy and feels that Lucy may be from the English branch of the Bojangles. But Daniel, the youngest of Hiram's five children, and a doctor, is very suspicious of Lucy's intentions . . .

Books by Joyce Johnson
in the Linford Romance Library:

JOYCE JOHNSON

TO WIN HER LOVE

Complete and Unabridged

LINFORD
Leicester

First published in Great Britain in 1997

First Linford Edition
published 2002

British Library CIP Data

Johnson, Joyce, *1931* –
    To win her love.—Large print ed.—
    Linford romance library
    1. Love stories
    2. Large type books
    I. Title
    813.5'4 [F]

ISBN 0–7089–9831–3

Published by
F. A. Thorpe (Publishing)
Anstey, Leicestershire

Set by Words & Graphics Ltd.
Anstey, Leicestershire
Printed and bound in Great Britain by
T. J. International Ltd., Padstow, Cornwall

This book is printed on acid-free paper

1

Lucy reversed neatly into one of the few remaining spaces in the Watson Rivers Company carpark, noted it seemed more crowded than normal, and felt again the nagging sense of foreboding that had dogged her since she'd left her cottage that morning.

Switching off the ignition, she closed her eyes in concentration and drew deep, calming breaths. Dr Norris had promised the attacks of panic-stricken premonitions of doom would become less frequent in time. And he'd been right. She was gradually coming to terms with the terrible tragedy which had wiped out her family — but whether she would ever pick up the threads of her life and put what had happened behind her was an entirely different matter.

And how much longer would that

part take? She remembered Dr Norris's words — 'Post traumatic stress, Lucy. It takes a long time to heal. You should have counselling, maybe leave Stonebridge for a while. A change of scene may at least help to soften the memories . . . '

'No, I can't leave. There's the cottage — it's all I have left. I'm going to restore it — live in it — I've nowhere else to go . . . '

'Whatever you think best,' Dr Norris had soothed. He'd known Lucy all her life and respected her innate commonsense. 'Follow your instincts and take a day at a time. You've a lot of support in the village — and friends . . . '

But no family any more. No farm to come home to, no prospect of ever working the land that had been in her family for generations. All her young life had been a preparation for that — running Hollowmead with her father and brother, Matt. She'd had just one more year of study at agricultural college . . .

2

Sharp taps on the car window broke into bitter memories of the past.

'Lucy, are you all right?'

She opened her eyes, forced a smile, and came back to the present. Picking up her briefcase, she stepped outside to join her friend, Fiona.

Fiona was an important member of her support group — and yet, there was still a barrier. Since the tragedy, she had built a wall around herself. People still treated her warily, some had even avoided her since the funerals. She knew they were embarrassed, especially since Peter had dealt her the final blow.

'I'm fine,' she reassured Fiona. 'I was just planning my bedroom.'

'You'll turn into a DIY bore if you're not careful, always on about wallpaper and three-piece suites. Unfortunately, it's Monday morning and we have to go back to work. The new school contract . . .'

'Practically done. We meet the Head tomorrow.'

After the events which had put paid

to her original career in farming, Lucy hadn't even finished her college course, much to the chagrin of her Principal. He'd done his best to persuade her.

'Leave it for twelve months. You're a fine student. Farming's been in your family for generations and it's in your blood. You'd sail through. You have to do something with your life.'

'Anything — except farming.'

She'd been positive, and when the funerals were over and affairs finalised, she'd applied for a sales job with Watson Rivers and found, to her relief, she had a talent for developing and selling software to schools and colleges. The job was her lifeline and slowly and painfully, she was managing to get back to some semblance of normality.

She followed Fiona into the main office building and knew at once that this time her morning's premonition was no idle fancy. Most of Watson Rivers staff were crowded into the reception area, all trying to read the main bulletin board.

4

'What's up?' Fiona, taller than Lucy, pushed her way to the front.

Voices were swift to tell them the bad news.

'There's going to be a takeover — an American company.'

'Merger.'

'I call it treachery.'

'Newcastle — they're going to relocate to Newcastle!'

The office manager's voice cut through the hubbub.

'Mr Watson's going to see everyone today. You've all got appointment times. But for now you should all get back to work.' He looked far from happy.

Lucy's forebodings increased throughout the long day as rumours multiplied. It was hard to concentrate on her job when her job might not even have a future.

The prevailing atmosphere was gloomy — many of the staff came out of Bill Watson's office clutching redundancy notices, shaking their heads in disbelief.

'A rotten trick. I thought better of Bill Watson. It's going to be really hard finding another job round here.'

Lucy was glad when it was her turn at three thirty. At least now she would know what was happening. Bill Watson looked drained and had long since run out of platitudes. He knew Lucy well, had been a friend of Matt's and the family.

'Lucy, you've read the letter I circulated. Watson Rivers have been taken over by Mallinsons of California.' He gestured towards two practically identical, tanned, blond-haired, athletic-looking men. 'Roger Mallinson and Harry Beam.'

Both men flashed smiles at Lucy. She found it impossible to smile back.

'Mallinsons want a base in the UK — and Watson Rivers will provide it,' Bill went on wearily. 'I'm really sorry. We'll be as generous as we can . . . '

'Within the terms of your employment law,' Harry Beam said smoothly. 'We're a business, not a charity, and

Miss . . . er . . . I see you've only been with the company twelve months.'

'How about joining us in Newcastle?' Bill said without much hope. 'Lucy's had a very difficult time recently.' He turned to the Americans who assumed a professionally sympathetic air — and looked at their watches.

'No thanks. I'm quite settled in the cottage, and on balance I believe I prefer Devon to Newcastle, but thanks for offering.' She held out her hand. 'Bill, I've enjoyed working for you. I'm sorry it's over. Good luck in Newcastle.'

Half an hour later, Fiona came out of the office with a thumbs-down sign.

'I'm out as well — with the offer of a one-way trip to Newcastle — which I turned down.' She shrugged. 'Happens all the time these days. Maybe I'll join Steve in Plymouth. We'll be living there anyway after we're married. I feel bad for you, Lucy — I know how much the job means.'

'As you say — happens all the time.' But this was yet another setback that

Lucy could well have done without.

'Let's go out for a drink tonight. Steve's coming down and we're having supper later. Why don't you come along, too?'

'Thanks — but I've an assignation — at the cottage.'

Fiona looked at her expectantly.

'Who?'

'The plumber. About the bathroom.' She laughed. 'Don't look so disappointed.'

'I just wish you'd start to get out and about a bit more. I know Pete gave you a rotten deal, but that was over a year ago . . .'

'It's still a bit soon . . . and I'm busy with the cottage. Tell you what, why don't you and Steve come to supper next week. I can show you the new bathroom!'

'Great. I'll bring Mike, that friend of Steve's we bumped into in town. I think he's pretty interested in you.'

'I'm not sure, Fiona. Nothing against Mike. He's nice.' But in her own head she added, 'But he isn't Pete!'

It was silly — why would she want to think of Pete after what he'd done to her and the way she'd been treated?

Yet she just couldn't bring herself to fall out of love with her ex-fiancé. He'd been such a part of her life — her old life, she had to keep reminding herself.

★   ★   ★

Like most of Watson Rivers' employees, Lucy had lots to think about on the drive home to her cottage on the other side of Stonebridge. She couldn't quite believe everything that had happened to her in recent times. She'd lost her family, fiancé, and now her job — all within the space of a year and a bit.

She rounded the bend and saw her cottage nestling in the dip before the road started its climb out of the village, and immediately felt better. Practically derelict when she moved in a year earlier, it was nearly transformed, externally at least, into a picture-book, idyllic, English country cottage.

It was a beautiful evening and she decided to work outside. There was a bit of rustic walling by the herb garden that needed seeing to. She'd change first, then do some work, have supper later and perhaps treat herself to a glass of wine. She reckoned she deserved it after the day's events.

Then she saw the man. Again! Not lurking this time, but blatantly strolling from the back of the cottage into the front garden — and, what a nerve, a camcorder on his shoulder!

'Hey — you. Stop that! You can't just barge in here and film my home. Go away.' She leaped out of her car, ran up the path and lunged at the camera, covering the lens. 'Stop it. I saw you on Saturday — peering over the hedge. What do you want?' She began to push him away, and then stepped back in alarm as he lowered the camera and came towards her.

She saw he was quite elderly, silver-haired, ramrod straight, and very

10

elegantly dressed — far too elegant for Stonebridge.

'Who are you? And what are you doing wandering in my garden?'

The man smiled and held out his hand.

'Pardon me. I'd no intention of alarming you, ma'am, or to be trespassing. Arnold B. Raste Senior, attorney at law, from USA — South Carolina.'

Lucy had already worked out he wasn't local, and with the tan and beautifully even white teeth, he couldn't be anything other than American.

'So why are you snooping around, spying on me?'

'It's so perfect.' He gestured at the cottage. 'Unless I take film they'll never believe it back home — right down to the honeysuckle and roses around the front door. And you, ma'am, if I may . . . ' He raised his camera. 'You are the perfect English rose in the perfect setting.'

Lucy jumped sideways out of focus, wondering if this was some kind of strange dream. She blushed.

'Nonsense. Please, stop it, go away or . . . or . . . I'll call the police.'

'Pardon me, ma'am. I'd forgotten. You English are a sight more formal than we are. I should have engineered a proper introduction. Guess I was carried away by all this — the lovely, enchanted summer evening . . . the cottage, and you, Miss Lucy Beaujangle.'

Lucy's irritation began to evaporate as Arnold B. Raste's old-fashioned, other-worldly charm poured oil on her jagged spirit. Then she recalled those other Americans who'd cost her her job. Her brows came together severely.

'And how exactly do you know my name? Are you connected with the Mallinson takeover?'

'Takeover? Mallinsons?' The cultured drawl was genuinely puzzled.

'Watson Rivers. Computer software.'

'Heaven forbid.' He raised his fine brown eyes to an orange-streaked sunset. 'I'm an attorney — property and estate. To me, computers are indecipherable. I leave all that to the junior partners. Watson Rivers? Sounds more like a clothing company. Who . . . or what, are they taking over?'

'It's the other . . . Oh, never mind. It doesn't matter,' she said tiredly.

'But I can see it does. You obviously haven't had a very good day today. You need a confidante — and Arnold B. Raste is here, at your service.'

'But you still haven't explained — and how do you know my name?'

Yet she felt her defences weakening — there was something appealing about Mr Raste, avuncular, comforting.

'Ma'am, if I might be allowed to see the inside of your charming cottage, you might care to discuss the . . . er . . . Watson Rivers situation. You have my word of honour as a Southern gentleman — my reputation is of the highest, my intentions the best. You are a most beautiful, young woman. You've a right to worry, but I believe I'm old enough to be your grandpappy, and you may telephone the Hare and Hounds, where I'm registered. They'll vouch for me.'

Lucy suppressed the urge to giggle.

He was a charmer, and actually made her feel light-hearted — for the first time in months. Old enough to be her grandpappy he may be but he certainly had a way with women.

'All right, you can come in. I'll even give you coffee — if you'll tell me why you're here.'

'I sure will, ma'am. Haven't I flown the Atlantic for that very purpose which concerns you closely — and I hate flying worse than I hate computers.'

Courteously he stood aside to allow her to precede him into the cottage. Arnold B. Raste Senior ducked his silver head under the living room lintel, straightened up smartly, and gasped in admiration.

'My, what a fine place!' His shrewd eyes swept the comfortable room. 'And some of those pieces. The dresser, and the corner cupboard. They're terrific, worth a fortune in the States. Heirlooms, I guess.'

'Yes — and not for sale. If you sit down, I'll get coffee.'

Her tone forbade further comment.

'Pardon me, ma'am. Out of turn again, I guess. I'll keep quiet a while.'

He sat down and folded his arms across his chest.

Waiting in the kitchen for coffee to brew, Lucy had time to consider her decision to invite him in. She must be going crazy — a stranger, and a foreigner! Probably head of a ring of antique furniture thieves. She'd forgotten how valuable some of the pieces were that she'd salvaged from the family home.

No doubt Arnold B. Raste, if that was his real name, was already totting up the value. She should have seen him off the premises at once — or called the police. And yet, there was something about him, a mystery, a purpose, he'd said, concerning her! She had to at least find out what tale he would spin as to the nature of that purpose.

When she took the coffee into the sitting room, she found the attorney studying a silver-framed photograph on the dresser. He put it down as she came into the room.

'Ma'am, let me take the tray for you. That your family? You and the boy, your brother, I assume, are as like as two peas.'

Lucy nodded, but her hands were shaking as she tried to pour the coffee. After all this time — it was ridiculous. The familiar constriction in the chest, the panic, the fear . . . but she couldn't just get rid of the photograph, couldn't erase the memory of her family, just because they were all dead. But would the agony ever stop? She carefully replaced the coffee pot on the tray, took a deep breath and waited for her hands to stop shaking.

'I'll do that, ma'am.' The tall American took charge. 'Drink this now. I shouldn't have picked up the picture — but I know what happened, Miss

Lucy, and I can tell you, I'm real sorry.'

'How do you know? And why?'

The coffee had a calming effect. Her hands steadied.

'I've been around Stonebridge a few days. Seems everybody knows everybody's business — and your family was well liked. Your tragedy shook up the whole place. Folks still talking about it. You don't need to tell me . . . '

Lucy leaned over and clutched his arm. She knew what was coming.

'But I do — that's the problem. It's awful, this compulsion. You know, I've got to go through it time and time again, even if they do know. People have been great, but there's a limit. I have to keep on, going over and over it, to anyone, strangers even. That's why I can't — can't go out . . . except to work . . . '

'So tell me, Lucy, if you need to — if it helps.'

'I don't know if it does, but I can't help it, and I certainly can't forget. I was away at college when it happened.

It was near the end of term and I was on a field trip in Scotland. If I'd been here, I could've helped. If Dad had told us . . . '

Her eyes glazed as she felt the familiar surge of words, as though someone had pulled a switch — she was on automatic. Arnold Raste covered her clenched hand with his.

'There had been a bumper harvest and storms were expected — they had to get it in. It was dusk and they really shouldn't've gone on. Matt got down from the harvester, there was an obstruction in the field. Dad, probably exhausted, certainly worried sick, lost control of the combine, a new one on hire from the cooperative — huge, high-tech, dangerous unless you were careful. Matt was walking ahead. He . . . ' She shut her eyes but her brain still flashed the pictures.

'Matt must have turned to wave Dad on. But looking over his shoulder, he must have seen the monster machine swinging down on him . . . and Dad

18

fighting for control. I don't know why Matt didn't jump away. He was caught up in the blades — '

She pushed her knuckles into her eyes and screamed, trying to obliterate the scenes which must have followed. There was silence in the cottage, a seemingly never-ending silence . . .

Arnold B. Raste removed his hand.

'Why do you torture yourself, ma'am? What purpose does it serve?'

He was matter-of-fact, almost unfriendly.

'Purpose? What's that to do with it? They're all gone. Don't you understand? My family — wiped out. One stupid error. If I'd been there . . . but by the time they contacted me, Dad had shot himself. Mum died a month later — of a broken heart. I never thought that was possible, except in fiction, but the autopsy could find nothing wrong with her — a normal, healthy woman.'

'You resent her for not staying — for you?' he cut in sharply. 'You continue to punish yourself because you feel guilty about that and about not being home? You have to grow up, Miss Lucy — get back to living. You don't even know if it happened like you imagine.' He paused, looked at the sad, tear-stained face before him, and took the plunge.

'You are guilty of the worst sin — hanging on to your tragedy, indulging yourself in constant self-pity. It'll kill you, too, in the end — if you don't let it go.'

The silence hung again between them, threatening. The red glow of sunset caught both old man and young girl through the leaded windows. The attorney unclasped Lucy's fingers from his arm and stood up.

'Ma'am, pardon me. I was wrong, I had no right . . . I think it best I leave. I spoke out of turn, but I thought maybe if I was blunt — it was most presumptuous of me.'

Slowly, she answered, her voice small and strained, as though it had travelled a hard and difficult route from her brain.

'Yes, Mr Raste, it was, it most certainly was.'

Her eyes stared past him at the fading sunset outside.

The attorney picked up his camera, hesitating by the door.

'Perhaps when you've had time to reflect and forgive me . . . a little . . . I may telephone you this evening?'

'Mr Raste, not only do I forgive you right now, I positively want to thank you for what you've just said. And if you think you're getting away without giving away a hint of your purpose here . . . ' Lucy's voice was stronger, confident, purposeful. 'What you said needed saying. No one's had the courage — and I haven't made it easy. You're right, I am guilty. Guilty of wallowing in my own selfish emotions, hiding from reality — the reality my family's truly gone. I had a wonderful upbringing — twenty-three happy years. I owe it to them to try to be happy. Mr Raste, you have wrought a miracle. I could — I could hug you.'

For the first time the lawyer's

sang-froid deserted him.

'Dear Miss Lucy . . . Do feel free, if you wish . . . '

She laughed. A great burden had lifted from her, an enormous lightening of the spirit. Dr Norris had told her there'd come a time — she hadn't believed him, but it was true.

'Don't worry, I shan't embarrass you — and I shan't break down again, or have hysterics. I guarantee it. Look.' She picked up the photograph of her lost family and touched the faces of her parents and brother. 'For the first time I can look at this and that . . . dreadful scene isn't triggered.'

'I'm glad.' He smiled. 'I took an unpardonable risk in speaking so frankly.'

'I'm grateful. Truly.'

'And a young girl as charming and attractive as yourself — I know it's small consolation now, but you'll have your own family one day! I cannot believe you don't have a string of suitors.'

Arnold B. Raste, Attorney, had to keep reminding himself he was there to do a job. It was all very well playing the counsellor to this lovely girl — he was being paid handsomely to work on someone else's behalf.

'No . . . er . . . partner?' he probed.

'Didn't your gossip source tell you? I was to be married the same year Matt and Dad died — after I finished college. A neighbouring farmer, Peter Dawson. We'd known each other since we were children. It seemed ideal! Both families would run the two farms together.

'Pete had it all worked out — he knew Dad would never sell and the only way he could get his hands on our land was by marrying me. He has ambitions to become a real county big-wheel in agriculture. What he didn't know — nobody did — was that Hollowmead farm was about to be declared bankrupt.

'That, as much as Matt's death, was why Dad killed himself. He couldn't share it — the burden, I mean. We'd all

23

have helped — it was so unnecessary to take his own life. I'm surprised the gossips didn't tell you that.'

Arnold B. Raste shook his head.

'Not a word, ma'am. Just the stark, dreadful facts.'

'Maybe they wanted to spare me the humiliation. You may as well know everything. What is it about you, Mr Raste? I've not talked so much for months.'

He spread his hands and gave an expressive shrug.

'Maybe because I'm a total stranger. Friends are sometimes too close for comfort, though I sure hope we'll become real good friends. So tell me now, what happened about Mr Dawson?'

'He seized his opportunity. When the farm went into liquidation, Pete snapped it up at a rock-bottom price. I truly think there was some deal with the receiver — not entirely above board, but at the time I was too distraught to care.

'So, instead of Pete being my pillar of

support, he just about kicked everything from under me! He also got married — a very rich girl from London. He has a baby son, born only last week, and there'll be lots more I expect. So I felt I'd lost that family, too. I was very much in love with Pete.' She said it in a very matter-of-fact way.

Was she truly still in love with him? Every time she drove past Hollowmead the knife twisted. Perhaps that, too, was part of the 'self inflicted torture' scenario Arnold Raste had punched a hole through. She truly hoped so.

'At least he sold me this cottage at a fairly reasonable price.'

'In the circumstances, less than gallant. He should have given it to you. Part of your family's property, I take it?'

'Yes. Dad planned to renovate it as a holiday cottage. Now I know why he didn't — there was no money! And another thing is, I can't even carry on the family name in their memory.'

'And a most unusual surname at that. In fact, it's what brought me to

Devon, England, and then to Stone-bridge.'

'My surname brought you here?'

'Yes, ma'am. I appreciate you telling me about your family. It kinda ties in with what I have to say.' He glanced at his watch. 'Miss Beaujangle . . . you've had a hell of a day — excuse me. Why not take a break, rest up a while, then I'll call back here for you in about an hour? Have dinner with me. The Hare and Hounds looks to have a fine menu. We can discuss my purpose in being here in relaxed surroundings. What do you say?'

'Oh, I couldn't . . . ' Lucy started to say, then thought, why not? It was an age since she'd been out to dinner. She'd got out of the habit and it was time she got back in again. She owed it to Mr Raste after the jolt he'd administered.

She thought for a second.

'I'd love to, but I'll drive myself. It's only a mile or so, and I'd prefer to be independent. I'll meet you in the bar,

26

eight sharp, and Mr Raste, what you have to say had better be interesting. This time I expect you to do the talking. I've talked enough to last me a lifetime.'

'It's a deal. I think you'll be interested, ma'am. You see, what I've come to offer is a . . . well, strangely, a new family, across the water — in South Carolina.' He took her hand, shook it, then touched it with his lips. 'You and I are going to be friends, I just know it. Already I feel I know you real well.'

Lucy's mouth hung open as she watched him go down the front path. A day of surprises — and they weren't over yet! She ran upstairs, mentally scanning her wardrobe. It was time to buy some new clothes, too. In her excitement, she completely forgot the plumber was due to call at any minute.

2

Arnold B. Raste eyed Lucy across the candlelit dinner table. He leaned forward and said quite loudly, 'That Peter Dawson is a jumping jackass and I don't care who knows it.'

'Ssh . . . ' Lucy glanced round. She knew several of the diners. They'd looked surprised to see her but had exchanged greetings, looking curiously at Mr Raste. She whispered, 'Why is he a jackass?'

'To pass up such a pretty girl as you — mad as a wild coyote!'

'Mr Raste, you're flattering me. We're here to talk business.' But Lucy was enjoying herself, too. She'd taken time and trouble with her appearance — her red-blonde hair was a shining, satin bell around her face, and the soft jade-green dress clung and touched her slim figure in just the right places.

Arnold Raste wore an even more elegant suit than before, and he treated Lucy like a princess, fashioned from priceless porcelain.

They ordered dinner.

'I just love your English steak and kidney pie — but I'm already homesick for my Carolina cooking.' He studied the menu.

'In what way is it different? I've never been to America, in fact, I haven't been anywhere very much.'

He closed his eyes for a second, then pursed his lips.

'Crab cakes, shrimp bisque, oyster pie, catfish stew with hushpuppies, country ham, blueberry cream pie . . .'

'Stop it.' Lucy laughed. 'It all sounds wonderful. I shan't be happy with my plain grilled salmon now. Perhaps I'll have the duck instead.' The waiter brought the wine, but she put her hand over her glass. 'I'm driving. Just a small one.'

'I'll send you home in a taxi.'

'I still have to get to work in the morning.'

'The boring Watson Rivers?'

'I don't find it boring, and I have to work out my notice.'

'May I ask you a personal question, Lucy?'

'I can't imagine I've many secrets left from you.'

'Are you short of money?'

She frowned and poked at the bread roll on her plate.

'Well, yes, I am, of course, but that really has nothing to do with you.'

'If I could offer you a job . . . ?'

'What sort of a job?' Her suspicions were alerted. Conversation with the American attorney had a tendency to swing out of control.

'Shall I explain now, or shall we enjoy our meal first?'

Lucy sighed.

'It really is time to explain yourself. At this rate I shall begin to suspect you don't have 'a purpose'. You're stalling again, Mr Raste.'

The waiter brought their first course, giving Arnold B. Raste a momentary

reprieve. Her perception was acute
— there was no fooling her. He was
stalling and had been since he'd got
back to the hotel and phoned Hiram
The Third. The old man had been none
too pleased.

'Quit dithering around. If you've
found her, bring her back here. What's
the hold-up?'

'She's had a rough time. I don't
know whether she's tough enough yet
to deal with you and yours.'

'Aw, don't talk hogwash. All I'm
proposing is an all expenses paid,
first-class vacation. What's wrong with
that, Arnold? She'll have a great time.
Fax me a picture — and all the details.
And get yourself back here ASAP, with
or without the Beaujangle. She can
follow. Got it?'

'Got it, Hiram,' the elegant Arnold
said, as the phone had gone dead. He
brought his attention back to Lucy who
was eating her first course with relish.

'Delicious fish soup. Bet it's better
than catfish stew. Start talking, Mr

Raste. Time's up!'

'Could you call me Arnold, perhaps? Mr Raste is so . . . so formal.'

'I'll call you anything you want just so long as you quit stalling. Now,' she said severely.

'Certainly. It's just . . . it's hard to know where to start.'

'The beginning!'

'Very well. It starts with Bojangle. Americanised Boj, not your Beau spelling. You've kept the French version mainly. I am Hiram Bojangle The Third's attorney . . . '

'There's a Hiram Bojangle? Hiram — the Third? I don't believe it!'

'It's not so funny. Hiram's a good American name.'

'I'm sorry, of course, but it's just . . . well . . . unusual. But please, go on.'

Arnold leaned back in his chair, all his attention focused on Lucy.

'Hiram Bojangle is very wealthy, a multi-millionaire. Old family, old money, from 'way back. Rice and indigo plantations in South Carolina

— around Charleston.'

'Charleston?' She sat up. 'I had a distant cousin who lived there, I believe. So Dad told me. We never made contact.'

'Do you have a family tree? Can you trace your ancestors far back?'

'Not really. Dad and Mum, and my grandparents, weren't terribly interested in that sort of thing. I just know there's been Beaujangles in this part of Devon for a long time — but gradually the families grew smaller and smaller. I'm the last now Matt's gone.' She swallowed back her sadness. 'It'd be wonderful to have some relatives now, however distant.'

'Do you have any family papers? Or bibles?'

'Not that I can recall. There's a whole load of stuff up in the roof at the cottage. I'll rummage about if it's important. You're not suggesting that I'm related to this Hiram the . . . er . . . Third?'

'Well, there may be a tenuous

connection — through the male line of course. No, it's Hiram, Mr Bojangle, who's tremendously interested in genealogy. He's got this notion about an English family branch, and he wants to see if there's a link. He is rather old, and this has become a matter of life and death to him.'

'What has?' Lucy eyed the duck breasts appreciatively and help herself to vegetables. It was hard to take the idea of a Hiram Bojangle III very seriously.

'He wants to see any distant Beaujangle before he dies. My brief was to contact anyone the detective agency we employed turned up with the surname Bo — or Beaujangle. You're the only genuine one, and Hiram wishes to see you.'

'You had me — the family — investigated! What a nerve!'

'Calm down, Lucy. It's perfectly in order. Missing persons . . . '

'I'm not a missing person. I'm here in Stonebridge. Have been all my life.'

'Hiram Bojangle is an old man. A very wealthy one. He has a whim. The old and wealthy can be a little odd, but they can afford to indulge their whims.'

'Not at my expense they can't. He's crazy. Why should I go halfway round the world to indulge a madman's whim? That's what you're suggesting, isn't it?'

Arnold B. Raste sighed. Lucy was a lovely and charming girl — Hiram would just adore her. But the English were so odd! So unpredictable. There she sat, glowering like a turkey cock ready for a fight. He slipped more wine discreetly into her glass.

'Now eat up your duck and listen. Let me tell you about Hiram's family . . .'

★ ★ ★

In Stonebridge, Devon, the summer day had been hot but pleasant with a cool breeze blowing in from the River Tamar. In Charleston, South Carolina, the summer day was relentlessly hot, and even the wind from the ocean failed to cut through the humidity.

Daniel, Hiram Bojangle's youngest son, dived cleanly into the huge kidney-shaped swimming pool and swam under water for as long as he could. Gasping, he eventually broke the surface, thankfully feeling the hot grime and sweat of his working day dissolve in the cool water.

The air conditioning at the county hospital had broken down yet again, and he'd operated through a long list in sweltering temperatures. The pool felt wonderful. He started to swim, a powerful crawl, easing away the day's tensions.

From his study on the third floor of the antebellum mansion which was the Bojangle residence, Hiram Bojangle III watched his youngest son, far below in the turquoise water and pondered the call from his attorney. He hoped Arnold wasn't losing his grip. Seemed to be making a vacation of it rather than getting on with the job. He brought his gnarled right fist down on his useless left arm. Damn it, but for this latest stroke, he'd have gone to England himself.

He leaned forward as a car swung around the wide, gravelled drive surrounding the house. It stopped by the pool and three young men got out dressed in immaculate tennis whites.

'Ducking work again — who the thunder's looking after things?' their father growled, wheeling himself nearer the window. He thrust his head forward, craned his neck like a bald-headed eagle prying on its young. One of the men squatted by the pool and spoke to Daniel.

'Guess they're trying to get him to make up a four.' The old man chuckled. 'Fat chance — he'll be off on some worthy do-good, no-good project or other.' He saw Daniel shake his head, smile, wave, and plunge back in the water. His older brother waved his racquet in disappointment and went back to the car. 'Told you!' Hiram said to the empty room. 'Always right. If only them darned boys'd take more notice of what I say.'

He moved back a little from the window, plucked with his right hand at the slipping rug round his knees, and clicked with frustration as it fell to the ground. If only he wasn't so helpless.

Pressing the button by the desk, he waited for one of the nurses to respond. Meanwhile, his eyes swept the acres of land beyond the pool and the tennis courts, drifted over the stables where the grooms were at work with his valuable stud horses. A sight of satisfaction escaped from his lips.

He'd done it all. Turned it around and kept it going in spite of everything. He frowned. In spite of everybody — in spite of those damned predatory women! He closed his eyes — he didn't have a lot of time left . . .

When the nurse came into the room, Hiram Bojangle was fast asleep, slumped ungraciously sideways in his wheelchair. His son, Daniel, dark hair still wet from his swim, followed the nurse and helped her straighten up the old man and tuck the rug around him. Daniel took his father's wrist, checked his pulse, put a hand to his forehead.

'Leave him to sleep, Paula. It'll do him as much good as medication. I'll be back later tonight.'

The nurse watched him pad away bare-footed across the thick carpet, the white towelling robe stark against muscular brown legs. She turned the wheelchair away from the window and wondered how the broken old shell that was Hiram Bojangle could have produced four such wonderful-looking sons. Dan was almost as good looking as Scott!

Of course, Nurse Paula was far too young to have known Hiram III in the full flush of his young manhood.

★ ★ ★

'So you see, Lucy, Hiram didn't have family until he was in his fifties. He was too busy reviving his fortune to look after his first two wives properly. He was generous enough, bought them anything their hearts desired, but he paid more attention to business matters — by necessity. The estates were pretty near bankrupt when he'd inherited them, and those two women made him pay in the end. He's still paying even now. Shall we have coffee in the lounge?'

'Yes, please. So all of his five children came from his last marriage?' Lucy, after her initial annoyance, was fascinated by Mr Raste's account of this fabulously wealthy, fairy-tale family with its affluent and cosmopolitan lifestyle.

Arnold nodded as they moved into the lounge to have coffee.

'Yup, his last wife, Ellie Pagett, was the love of his life. Thirty years younger than Hiram, she gave him five children and the happiest years of his life.

Unfortunately she died ten years ago. Then, five years later, Hiram had his first stroke. He's confined to a wheelchair which, for such an active man, is purgatory. That's when he became interested, quite fanatically so, in genealogy. The idea of the English connection fascinated him and, as I said, it became an obsession to trace any descendants.'

'But if he's got this wonderful family in Charleston, isn't that enough? Why bother with a very remote connection here in the West Country? I'm sorry I was cross at first, but it just seemed . . . well, so bizarre.'

'I can understand that, but the old have a different way of looking at things. Family, past history, maybe gives them a sense of continuity, permanence . . . '

'Do you feel that, Arnold? Have you a family?'

'A son — in New York. Two grandchildren. My roots are in Charleston.'

'Wife?'

'Thankfully — we are both still alive and together — after forty years. When you come to Charleston, you and Joelle will love each other instantly.'

The English didn't usually love strangers right away, and yet here she was with Arnold B. Raste, known him less than six hours, and already he seemed part of her life!

'Mr . . . Arnold, I must go. The time's flown. I've had a lovely dinner and I've enjoyed being with you. Perhaps you'll eat with me tomorrow at the cottage. You can tell me more about the Bojangles.'

'Nothing would give me greater pleasure, ma'am, but I have to fly back to the States tomorrow. Pressing legal matters are about to overwhelm me unless I return.'

'Oh I thought . . . ' Disappointment sank her spirits.

'You could fly back with me.' He eyed her intently. 'I travel first class. Hiram is generous with expenses.

Another ticket is only a phone call away.'

'Goodness me, I couldn't possibly go to America tomorrow.'

The attorney emptied the coffee pot and summoned the waiter for a refill.

'Just an academic question, Lucy. Why not?'

'Why not? Er, well, I'm still working for a start. I've an appointment tomorrow.'

'From the sound of it, your Watson Rivers have forfeited any right to your loyalty.'

'Bill Watson gave me a job which I desperately needed at the time. It's a personal debt — nothing to do with Mallinsons Incorporated.'

'All right. But I could delay my flight a day or so — if you would accompany me. I can rearrange my pressing affairs by phone and fax. I'm sure you could do the same . . . '

'My hair needs cutting.' Lucy put her hand to her hair.

He looked bewildered.

'Your hair is perfect — and I expect Joelle could find you an adequate replacement. We do have hairdressers in the States, you know!'

'But it's not the same. And . . . ' Her hand flew to her mouth. 'Oh, no, I couldn't possibly!'

'What? What is it?' Lucy's face was so tragic, Arnold feared the worst, hysteria about to break out again, tragic memories resurfacing?

She took her diary from her bag and began flicking pages.

'The plumber's coming back in a week to do the bathroom.'

'I'm sorry?' Arnold was completely mystified.

'The bathroom — I'm getting a new one. It's a big job — I need to be here to oversee it, so you see, it's out of the question. You make it sound wonderful, Arnold — a fairy tale, but I've got to get on with my life here in Stonebridge.'

Arnold B. Raste saw his guest to her car, then faxed a note to his employer.

He prided himself in being a good judge of character, and was confident in the message he sent.

Returning tomorrow 20th as scheduled — without Beaujangle. She follows soonest. Arnold B. Raste.

Duty done, he ordered a large whisky, took it up to his room and settled down for a long and expensive transatlantic chat with his dear wife, Joelle. He had lots to tell her, and Hiram never queried his telephone expenses, especially calls to Joelle!

3

Excitement rose in Lucy as the British Airways 767 approached Charlotte International Airport, North Carolina. She wasn't much travelled, unlike many of her contemporaries who seemed endlessly to be roaming Europe, the States, Australia, for weeks every summer. Pete had promised an exotic honeymoon and had often accused her of being a stick-in-the-mud home-bird.

Unadventurous, probably his synonym for boring, Lucy thought as the wheels bumped on to the runway. Well, not any more. Lucy Beaujangle was newly transformed into an adventuress, ready for anything!

Arnold B. Raste had judged correctly. Lucy's flat denial had been a play for time — time to digest his astonishing proposal. Even as she drove home that night after dinner, it wasn't the new

46

bathroom she had in mind. It was the attorney's evocative description of South Carolina and the lure of a change of scene which began to bite.

And maybe it was time she stepped out of her tight, little corner to explore what was beyond the horizons of Devon and England.

'It's the chance of a lifetime — you'd be a fool to miss it. You've nothing to lose — just go,' Fiona had urged.

Still she'd hesitated, until the letter arrived. The envelope stamped, *Raste and Wilmot, Attorneys at Law, Charleston, S. Carolina*, containing a first-class open return air flight from Gatwick to Charlotte and a banker's draft for what to Lucy was a staggering amount of dollars. A note inside simply said, *Everyone at Bojangle Plantation looks forward to your visit.*

The signature, straggled weakly across the paper was, *Hiram Bojangle III and family.*

That very same evening Arnold Raste had telephoned, sweeping Lucy into acquiescence with firm authority, putting the matter beyond doubt by bringing an ally to the phone.

'Lucy, dear? I'm Arnold's wife, Joelle. He's told me so much about you that I'm quite jealous! There's no question, I've got to meet you. If you're worried about the Bojangles, you come anyway and spend a wonderful vacation at our home. The way Arnold describes you is just the daughter I've always longed for. I just can't wait to meet you.'

The genuine warmth in the rich, Southern voice was overwhelming. Lucy decided that if Americans did have a tendency to go over the top, she liked it!

When she'd finished speaking to Lucy, Joelle Raste put the phone down and looked sternly at her husband.

'Now, you assure me, Arnold, that those Bojangles aren't bringing that girl over here just to make a fool of her — some crazy notion of Hiram's that'll frighten her half to death.'

'Joelle, I've never in over forty years

of marriage lied to you. I swear, as far as I know, Hiram simply wants to see the girl because he's got this notion about the British family connection. Eccentric — but harmless!'

Joelle looked unconvinced. Her husband had been the Bojangle lawyer too long for her not to be wary of Hiram's schemes and plots.

'That had better be the case — and you and I will just have to keep an eye on her. I don't trust Hiram. Ever since Ellie died . . . '

'It'll be a pleasure for both of us to make sure Lucy Beaujangle comes to no harm. Now, just stop worrying, nothing's going to happen to Lucy. Anyway, what possible harm could befall her? We'll see to it she has a wonderful time. I don't think she's been abroad much, and never to the States.'

'Are we to meet her at Charlotte and drive her down? I'd like that.'

'No. Hiram's fixed for one of the boys to fly down and pick her up.'

'Which one?'

'I don't think Hiram's decided yet.'
Joelle Raste frowned.

'Maybe I'll pay Hiram a visit tomorrow.'

Lucy's first-class ticket ensured she was whisked off the plane almost as soon as it touched down and that she was first past Immigration. As soon as she stepped into the VIP arrival lounge, a tall man, casually dressed in shorts and a T-shirt came to meet her, hand outstretched, smiling broadly.

'Lucy Beaujangle? Hi. I'm Hiram Bojangle Junior. Mighty pleased to meet you. Good flight?' He took her hand luggage and looked her over approvingly. 'Arnold's told us all about you — recognised you right away from his description. Pretty as an English rose, he said! Come on now.'

She knew it! Even white teeth and a wonderful tan, but dark hair not blond. She was glad of that. Also a very long stride she had difficulty keeping up with.

'Shouldn't I get my luggage?'

'That'll be loaded on to my plane. Should be about done now.'

'Your plane?' Lucy couldn't help the awed squeak.

Hiram Junior looked surprised.

'Didn't Arnold tell you you'd be met and flown on to Charleston?'

'Met, yes, but . . . er . . . I thought maybe a car . . . '

'Only way to travel, ma'am. Most folk around where we live have their own planes.'

'I agree,' Lucy said straight-faced, and decided to enjoy every new experience and put aside her English puritan streak. Hadn't she accepted Hiram's money — and the first-class ticket Fiona had dared her refuse at her peril? In less than half an hour she was airborne again.

'Enjoying the ride?' Hiram grinned. 'Want to take the controls for a spell?'

'Goodness, no — thank you. I'm having fun just watching you. It's amazingly comfortable.'

He laughed.

'It's not the Number One in the fleet. Scott needed that to take a business party to Savannah yesterday. That's a twenty-seater. This is just a baby — six seater.' Hiram Junior leaned back and pointed to a cold box strapped on a rear seat. 'There's cold drinks and food in there if you're hungry. Champagne if you want it, though there'll be plenty of that later. Whole family's turning out to meet you at a special dinner — plus Arnold and Joelle, of course.'

Lucy was relieved to hear Arnold would be there.

'Yes, Dad's giving a real shindig — gotta whole new lease of life since you gave him the OK.'

'I didn't . . .'

'Yup. Even young Daniel's been commanded to turn up. Presidential summons — not to be ignored!'

'Daniel?'

'Youngest male of the present Bojangles. Very youngest is Lisa — she's eighteen. Dan's a doctor. Not too delirious about family gatherings.

Tried to slither out of this one. Said he was on call at the hospital, so Dad phoned the Chief Administrator. Daniel was hopping mad I can tell you, but as the Bojangle Foundation supports the hospital practically single-handed, the Chief Executive wouldn't have Dan on duty at any price.

'But you take no notice of Daniel — he can be mighty cussed at times. We'll take care of you. Don't even need to see him after tonight. He's hardly ever at the plantation.' His blue-eyed smile was attractive, warm and friendly.

Lucy smiled back.

'Gee, Arnold certainly picked a good one!' He patted her shoulder. 'I sure hope we're going to be good friends.'

'I . . . hope so.' Lucy found Hiram's deep direct and definitely interested gaze unnerving, and injected a cool touch of frost in her reply. The last thing she wanted was any sort of involvement with the younger Bojangles! She looked down at the unfamiliar landscape and drew a breath.

The plane was following a series of lakes and inlets against lush green countryside. Ahead, in the far distance, she could see the blue ocean waters, but it was the grandeur of the white houses below which caught her breath.

Hiram touched her arm.

'Buckle up, we're about to land. There's the Palmetto Plantation. See, due south of us — mile or so ahead. There's the airstrip runway.'

'You mean you've got your own?'

Hiram's answer was to touch down with the gentlest of bumps. The plane slowed as he slewed it round to a halt just yards from a waiting limousine. He unstrapped his belt and took off his headset.

'Here's the welcoming party — right on the button.'

Lucy saw two men and a girl get out of the car and look towards the plane. One of the men had his hand on the girl's shoulder, and the three of them seemed to be arguing fiercely. The taller of the two men jerked his head towards the aircraft and the girl tried to pull away from the restraining hand of the other.

'Lucy.' Hiram was at the door of the plane looking expectantly at her. 'Aren't you coming?'

'Of course.' She turned away from the window, unbuckled, and followed him, trying to shrug off a twinge of nervous apprehension.

Hiram stepped on to the grass and helped her down. He kept her hand in his and led her over to the car.

'Here she is, guys, Miss Lucy Beaujangle, come to visit her transatlantic cousins.'

'I hardly think . . . we don't know for sure . . . ' But her words were lost in a flurry of welcoming handshakes and greetings as they stepped forward one by one.

'Scott Bojangle. Pleased to have you in South Carolina, Lucy.' The tall American was a younger version of Hiram Junior.

'Corey Bojangle. Great to have you here.' A shorter, fairer version pumped her hand.

'Lisa.' The dark-haired young girl took both of Lucy's hands in hers. 'At last, female reinforcements! I've longed for you to get here.'

Lucy's nervousness evaporated in the warmth of their friendliness as she leaned back against the soft, leather upholstery of the luxurious limousine, and breathed a sigh of relief. It was all going to be fine! No doubt of it. The Bojangles were delighted to see her. They kept up an enthusiastic barrage of questions and information.

'Do you play tennis?' Scott, who was driving, spoke over his shoulder as they drove past two immaculate courts, one grass, one shale.

'A little. I'm not very good.' Her eyes swivelled as she took in the sweeping lawns, landscaped parklands, trees and shrubs, the shimmer of a large lake in the distance.

'Scott and Corey are addicts.' Lisa's Southern drawl was more pronounced than her brothers'. 'They'll have you out on the courts whatever you say. They're good enough to be professionals.'

'But fortunately we don't need the money!' Scott laughed.

'What do you all do then?' Lucy ventured, feeling overwhelmed by all the affluence surrounding her.

'We three work on the family estates, here and in Savannah. We've got property — business interests. Lisa here's just decorative.'

'I'm not. I . . . I work just as hard as you.' She stared at her brothers fiercely and tossed back her sleek, dark bob of hair.

'Ugh! Call that stuff work? Damn fool ideas of Dan's. Stupid slave labour, and for what?' Corey was scornful.

Hiram interrupted calmly. 'No quarrelling. We have a guest, remember!'

Lucy sensed the crackle of antagonism.

'Families, Lucy! You know how they are?' Hiram managed to defuse the tension.

Family. The word still hurt, but her cry of astonishment at the scene ahead was involuntary.

'Quite something, huh?' Hiram looked pleased.

A wide avenue of mossed oaks stood as guardian sentinels leading to a most magnificent house. The white colonnaded portico entrance rose imposingly to three-storey height; wide verandas ran the length and width of the mansion like wedding-cake tiers. Three flags flew from the first-storey balcony.

Scott followed her gaze.

'American, South Carolinian with the palmetto palm, and the pineapple is our welcome flag, 'specially for you, Lucy.'

Corey jumped out, opened the door, and helped her out with a bow.

'Welcome to the Bojangle Plantation, ma'am. Part of your ancestry, too.'

Previously, Lucy had believed characters were only rendered speechless in novels — now she knew it to be possible. She stood at the base of the marble steps leading to the front doors of the house and gaped at its magnificence.

Lisa took her arm.

'Come on, Daddy'll be waiting for you. I'll show you round later.'

As she spoke the massive double doors were flung open to frame an old man in a wheelchair flanked by two nurses, both in white. The man in the chair tried to rise in greeting but a firm hand on his shoulder forced him back, and Lucy saw the fourth person in the group standing directly behind the invalid's chair.

Dark hair, brown eyes, tall, broad-shouldered, and the same strong features as the other male Bojangles. She guessed this was the reluctant Daniel. At least he didn't have the regulation U.S. tan. But she did wonder why not.

She heard him say, 'No need to overdo it, Father. They'll come to you.'

The Southern accent, Lucy decided, was the most captivating in the world. Daniel's voice was pure molasses, velvety rich.

The group waited at the top of the steps. Lisa ushered Lucy up into the entrance hall and Hiram Bojangle III stretched out a brown-spotted hand.

'Lucy Beaujangle, ma'am, a pleasure to receive you here at the plantation. I hope you'll have a real good visit with us — our hospitality will be gravely at fault if you don't. Come in where I can see you. Dan, wheel me over to the window. My youngest son, Daniel.' He waved a cursory introduction and Daniel nodded.

Lucy noted he didn't smile, though the faint crinkles and the upturned curve of his mouth indicated he frequently did.

'Welcome to the Palmetto Plantation, Miss Beaujangle.' His tone was even, the eyes wary. He pushed the chair across the polished, wooden floor into a sitting room and Lucy was aware of fine furniture, rich hangings and china.

The old man still held her hand, leading her to a wide circular window.

'Blinds,' he snapped.

The male nurse leaped to obey and sunlight flooded the room. Hiram Senior blinked, pulled Lucy nearer to him, scanned her face, then released her.

'Hmm, can't see any family resemblance there. Pure English rose!'

'Dad.' Hiram Junior went over to the wheelchair. 'It was over three centuries ago the Beaujangles left England. Any connection's bound to be pretty diluted.'

'I know that. I'm not the fool you think this stroke's made me.' He tapped his head. 'Still an active brain in there and don't you forget it.' He glared at his family, but smiled at Lucy. 'Did you bring the papers Arnold told me about?'

'Yes. I went through all the old stuff I brought from the farm. I don't expect it'll be much use, though I did find an old family Bible. Goes back a generation or two . . . '

'Excellent, excellent.' The old man's eyes lit up. 'Where . . . ?'

'Lucy's hardly had time to unpack, Daddy,' Lisa said, 'and she must be tired after her flight. Give her a chance.'

Hiram's face softened and he patted his daughter's arm.

'You're right. I'm a selfish, old man, but it's important, d'you see?' He turned to Lucy. 'At my age you don't have much time and what with all this . . . '

He suddenly looked immensely frail and Daniel gestured to the nurses.

'Dad, you should take your medication now, and rest. You've been keyed up all day. Now she . . . Lucy's here you can relax. Rest up for your celebration dinner tonight.' His tone was disapproving and Lucy remembered what Hiram Junior had said. ' . . . not too delirious about family gatherings.'

'All right, all right.' Hiram Senior was testy again. 'I'll do as I'm told but . . . ' He looked pleadingly at Lucy. 'If you could, ma'am, I'd be grateful if you could rustle up those papers, and the Bible, straight away. Lisa, you go with

Lucy and then take the documents to Clark — he's the genealogist I've hired to trace your family line, Lucy. He's been working on it since Arnold tracked you down in Devon, England.'

'But I don't understand. Of course I'm very grateful to be here. It was very generous to invite me . . . but why do you want to trace my line?'

The old man tried to assume a bland expression but the pucker of his mouth from the stroke made it hard for him to look anything but slightly sinister.

'Just a whim, girl, just a whim. Indulge an old man.' He smiled. Brown eyes, like Daniel's, and for the first time Lucy had a fleeting glimpse of a dashing younger man, then it vanished and the querulous, old man returned as he banged a stick impatiently on the floor.

'Besides, ain't it natural to want pretty, young things about me while I've the chance?' He pointed his stick at Lucy before laying it across his knees. 'Hope you've brought your best bib and tucker for tonight. I want everyone in full rig and that's an order,' he barked as the nurse wheeled him away.

His sons and daughter raised their eyes heavenwards and glanced at each other. Daniel looked at Lucy and seemed about to speak but Hiram Junior frowned.

'You heard, Daniel — full evening rig — and that includes you.'

'I don't see why.' He glared at his brother then turned on his heel. 'Oh, what's the use? I'm going for a swim.'

'Perhaps Lucy would like . . . ' Lisa began, but Daniel had gone.

'Leave him. He'll work it off — he'll be at dinner. Lisa, will you show Lucy to her suite, and don't forget to take the papers for Clark.' Hiram smiled. 'We're all looking forward to dinner — a real family occasion.'

4

For a few sleep-sodden seconds Lucy felt the familiar wave of panic in her stomach as the disembodied voice floated through the mesh screen of her bedroom window. 'Family!' The word again. It had shocked her into waking. Leaning back against the thick velvet headboard she struggled to reorientate herself. The voice rose again, tinged with exasperation.

'Honey, you know I can't come over, and neither can you come here. I've told you over and over, it's family only except for Arnold and Joelle, and they're pretty well family, since Mom died. No, I don't know what Dad's up to . . . but we have to go along with it. Don't be silly, Carol, you know why . . . '

Lucy's sumptuous guest suite over-looked the pool area and she guessed that's where the voice came from. Daniel was the swimmer but she was sure it wasn't his voice — his was deeper by a tone or two. Scott? Corey? The shades were electronically controlled from the bedside. Her finger hesitated over the switch as she heard her name.

'Lucy? Yeah, she's here . . . coupla hours ago. How do I know what she's doing? Resting up before the ordeal by dinner, I guess. What? No! Only family I said. You don't qualify, and never can — not while the old man's alive. The girl? Kinda pretty . . . English type with blondish hair. Carol, if you gatecrash tonight we're through, I mean it. I can't afford to upset Dad right now . . . ' There was a pause and Lucy pushed the button, and as the window shades sashayed softly down she heard, 'I'll be along later tonight if I can get away . . . '

She grabbed her watch — quarter to seven! Ordeal by dinner at seven fifteen for seven thirty — not enough time to ponder on the angry Carol. There was a discreet knock and a young woman's head came round the door.

'I've run your bath, ma'am. Mr Hiram hates for guests to be late. D'you want any help dressing?'

'Goodness no. Thanks though.' She softened the refusal with a smile. 'I'm used to managing myself. Maybe you could check me over when I'm done . . . see if I'm grand enough?'

'I'm sure you'll look lovely. Is this the dress?' The woman touched the dark, midnight-blue silk hanging in the enormous closet connecting bed and bathroom. 'It's beautiful.'

'Yes — it's my only smart frock.' Meant for my exotic honeymoon with Pete, Lucy thought ruefully — bought before the accident. 'I haven't worn it yet.'

Mr Hiram's welcome dinner for you is a good time to wear it then. I'll pop back in ten minutes just to check you've got everything.'

★   ★   ★

67

Lucy shook her head at the discreetly hovering wine waiter — she'd already drunk two glasses of champagne. Her body clock was still at UK time, and a floating sense of unreality was setting in. She fought a strong desire to lay her head on the elaborate table setting and fall fast asleep.

Hiram III dominated the proceedings from his wheelchair at the table head; Lucy sat on his right, Hiram IV on his left. All the men except Daniel wore white tuxedos and black ties. Daniel conceded a light grey suit and open-neck shirt and ignored his father's grumblings.

Joelle Raste played hostess from the other end of the table. She'd greeted Lucy with affectionate warmth and the promise that the two of them would get along just fine, both being Scorpios. Lucy had liked her right away.

Clark Haines, Hiram's genealogist, was an earnest, young man who'd quizzed her about her ancestors before dinner.

'You're sure you don't have your grandparents' birth certificates any-where?'

'I'm sorry, Clark. I wish I'd been more organised, but I never really thought about it before. We were always so busy on the farm.'

'Records, Haines, records! All the information's there — you just dig it up. A scholarly attitude, diligence, and a keen interest. You do the first two and I'll take care of the latter — and provide the cash of course.' Hiram patted Lucy's hand.

'Arnold told me all about your family. We're all real sorry. But don't you worry. There's a new family right here for you, ain't that so, Arnold?'

The attorney, splendidly elegant in his tuxedo, looked non-committal.

It was Joelle who said, 'Don't be in such a rush. Lucy's only been here five minutes. Give her time to find her feet and get used to you all.'

Hiram raised his hands.

'All right — a day to settle in and

enjoy the place. It's got just about everything you could ever want. The family'll take good care of you, show you around — and that's an order,' he growled at them. 'You report back to me if they don't, Lucy. They got little enough work to do . . . '

A chorus of protest from everyone except Daniel, who merely smiled at his father, and shook his head warningly at Lisa who'd gone an angry scarlet.

'That isn't fair, Daddy. Dan works every hour of the day — and night sometimes. If it's not the hospital it's . . . '

'Aw, that's not work — that loony do-gooder project . . . ' Corey sneered at his younger brother across the table. 'Just because you're a surgeon you don't think business counts for much . . . '

'Of course I do. It's hard to forget it when it's Bojangle dollars financing the hospital.'

'I notice you don't turn them down.'

70

The younger Hiram banged his fork on the plate.

'Enough!' Hiram Senior whipcracked from his chair, and the rising argument subsided. But the tension was bouncing off the walls.

Lucy had felt it in the car from the airstrip, and reckoned intuitively the united Bojangle front was a fairly fragile structure! Not for the first time she wondered what she was doing there within that structure.

'We have a special guest from England tonight,' Hiram Senior rasped. 'Show some respect.'

'Lucy, dear, perhaps you and Lisa'd come shopping with me tomorrow. Charleston has some lovely stores.' Joelle poured soothing oil on the increasingly troubled waters.

'Save time for some tennis coaching.' Lisa leaned across and a babble of conversation patched over the cracks. But it was stilted and awkward, and Lucy was relieved when Daniel stood up and threw down his napkin.

'Dad, I'm sure Lucy feels good and welcome, but it's time for your medication, and it's been a long day. I'll take you up. Joelle, would you see to coffee — in the conservatory maybe?'

'Sure. Be glad to. Goodnight, Hiram, dear. Don't you overdo things now.'

'Ugh. Chance'd be a fine thing.' But the bark was fading and Hiram Bojangle Senior, suddenly looking very tired, allowed himself to be wheeled away by his broad-shouldered son.

'Lisa,' Daniel said to his sister, 'can you come, too? I want a word.'

With the removal of the old man, the rest of the party visibly relaxed and coffee was an informal, laid-back affair, in contrast to the grand dinner! Joelle and Arnold told Lucy a little of the history of the area, promising to take her out on their boat on a harbour tour.

Later, after Scott and Corey had left, Lucy found it was getting harder to conceal her yawns, her eyelids fluttering closed once or twice.

'Lucy! How thoughtless of us.' Joelle jumped up. 'You must be exhausted. Let the poor child get to bed. Arnold, come along. Say thank you for dinner to your father, Hiram, and leave Lucy to get some rest.'

'We'll walk you to your car. Coming, Lucy?'

Lucy would much rather have walked herself to bed, but the evening air was still deliciously balmy and reviving, and once they'd seen off Arnold and Joelle she began to wake up a little.

'Like to see the lake?' Hiram asked. 'The path's floodlit and it's mighty pretty down there in the moonlight . . . but if you're too tired . . .'

'No, I'm fine.' Politeness won over fatigue and Hiram took her arm and led her on to a wooden jetty where several boats were moored.

'The lake leads down to the coast. It's a pretty sail. I'll take you soon.' He turned to lean against the rail. 'How long you planning to stay, Lucy?'

'I don't know. Your father sent me an

open ticket. It was very generous.'

'Father'll stop at nothing when he wants something, and money's no object.'

'Hiram, what does he want from me?'

'No more than a whim, he says — trace the Bojangle English connections, and it seems that's you. I don't much care about that but it brought you here. That's good enough for me.' He moved closer and Lucy found herself pinned between the jetty rail and Hiram's athletic body. He touched her hair.

'That looks wonderful in the moonlight. You're a mighty attractive woman, Lucy. I sure hope Clark don't prove we're very close relations!' His face was very near hers; his intention obvious.

He was attractive, very masculine, and Lucy's hurt pride was ready for some healing, but she side-stepped neatly and shivered a little.

'I think I should go back now. It's been a long day, and you and Scott

74

promised me a tennis lesson in the morning.'

'OK, you call the shots. Early days, I guess.' He tucked her arm in his and walked her back up to the mansion, many of its windows with lights still blazing.

'It's a fairy tale,' Lucy breathed. 'Magic!'

'So are you, Miss Beaujangle. That dress . . . wowee!' He put his arms around her and kissed her. It was a light and friendly kiss and Lucy didn't move away. Lucy returned the gesture by kissing him on the cheek.

'I shouldn't do that too often,' he warned. 'Could be dangerous.'

She giggled, the floating feeling of extreme tiredness making her light-headed.

'Aren't any of you married? You are all . . . very personable . . . '

'Oh, sure . . . and rich.' His confidence was all-American and Lucy considered she needn't have chosen her words so carefully!

'Let's just say we're all between marriages just for the present. We might have . . . what do you call it in England . . . silver spoons in our mouths . . . but we've sure hit the dregs over women — no disrespect, ma'am.'

'You've been married?' How naïve she'd been. Hiram was at least in his mid-thirties . . . and wealthy — they all were.

'Twice.' His face closed.

'Oh,' was all Lucy could say. 'I'm sorry.'

'Don't be. I'm paying for it. Just haven't met the right kinda woman,' he added significantly, 'yet!' He put his hands on her shoulders and looked deeply into her eyes. 'Hope you're going to be around a while, Lucy. I'm looking forward to us getting better acquainted.'

'I . . . I really must go to bed.' She regretted her earlier flirtatiousness.

'OK. See you in the morning then.'

Hiram Junior was looking forward to the time Lucy would spend with them all.

Back in the quiet luxury of her rooms Lucy perversely found herself wide awake, restless, yet gritty-eyed from lack of sleep. She made some tea — there was beautiful fine china in the compact kitchenette.

It was all wonderful, yet . . . nagging unease settled in the pit of her stomach. There was a lot of tension in the house — a tension the old man's presence seemed to exacerbate. Or maybe the Bojangles were just an ordinary, mega-rich American family and she had an over-heated imagination.

Sighing heavily, she looked out of the window. The pool was still lit. Lisa had shown her the covered way down from the suite. Exercise — that's what she needed — action after all that sitting on the plane, being polite at dinner!

She pulled on a swimsuit and grabbed a towel. All the lights were still on and the water looked marvellous. A running dive and she was under the water, striking out strongly, feeling the tensions of the day draining out of her.

Surfacing, she swam length after length.

Finally relaxed, she was ready for sleep. Just one more time . . . she turned and floated, eyes closed, drifting, letting the water take her . . . sinking.

'Hey!' There was a great splash by her side, a hand shaking her. 'Hey, Lucy, come on — don't go to sleep. How stupid can you get?'

She trod water, shaking her hair out of her eyes.

'I'm not . . . I wasn't . . . let go . . . ' His hand was still on her back, sliding down to her waist, supporting her to the side. 'I'm all right,' she persisted crossly. 'There's no need to push me.'

Daniel more or less hauled her out of the pool, on to one of the loungers by the side. He threw her a towel.

'Bit late for a swim . . . '

'I couldn't sleep. You don't mind, do you?'

He shook himself, droplets of water spraying from his body. He rubbed his dark hair and looked coolly at her.

'No, I don't mind at all. Guilty conscience?'

'What?'

'Keeping you from sleeping? You must be dog tired.'

His legs were long, hard and muscular. He was the tallest of the brothers. How many times had he been married? She daren't ask — there was something aloof and self-contained about this Bojangle. She wasn't prepared to risk a sarcastic put-down at this time of night.

'Why should I have a guilty conscience?' She combed her wet hair with her fingers and wrapped the towel more tightly round her.

He shrugged. 'I wouldn't know — yet! How long . . . ?'

'Am I planning to stay? That's the second time I've been asked. Do you usually ask visitors when they're leaving — as soon as they arrive?'

'Yes. I saw you out there with Hiram.' He ignored her question. 'No work deadline in England . . . unlimited time off?'

'No — though it's none of your business.' His cool questioning annoyed her. 'I don't have a job at present. I . . . '

'Ah, I see. Well, if you've done here . . . ' He moved to a master switch near the changing rooms. 'Unless you plan another length or two — though I don't advise it. You'd probably fall asleep and drown.'

His tone implied he wouldn't be too upset if that happened.

Lucy opened her mouth to argue, then thought better of it. What was the point? For some reason this youngest Bojangle had taken a dislike to her. If she remembered correctly he wasn't around much, so that shouldn't bother her. But oddly enough, it did!

She looked at him, his hand still on the switch, waiting for her to leave. His dark eyes were plainly saying she was an interloper and had no place there — or anywhere else at Palmetto Plantation.

'I'm going.' She was brusque. She was hardly out of the pool area and into the corridor leading to the house when the pool area was plunged into darkness.

Hurrying back to her suite, she wondered what on earth she'd let herself in for, yet strangely, she felt neither panic nor anxiety — merely a challenging sense of exhilaration. At least it was all a very different world! Yawning prodigiously she climbed into the king-size bed and switched off the bedside lamps.

'Absolutely right, Doctor Norris,' she said into the soft darkness, 'a change of scene indeed. Maybe I should've left Stonebridge months ago.'

5

'That was great!' Flushed and out of breath, Lucy reined in her horse beside Lisa's after a furious gallop across the open country.

'You're no novice on a horse, Lucy.' Lisa leaned down and patted her mare's steaming flank.

'Don't forget, I was brought up on a farm.' She could talk about the farm and her family now — the relief of not feeling that unremitting pain of agonising loss was wonderful. There was still sadness, but it was manageable.

'You had your own horse, I guess?'

'Bangle. Silly name! Matt christened her Beaujangle Bangle. As kids we thought that was hilarious. We were always teased about our surname so we had to turn the joke on ourselves at every opportunity.'

'It's a great name. I'm real proud of

it — and best of all, it brought you to Palmetto. We all just love having you.'

'Mmm, thanks.' Lucy still couldn't get used to the extrovert enthusiasm which seemed so much part of the American character. She did try — and it was getting easier. With one exception, everyone was so open and friendly it was easy to respond in kind.

'Best walk the horses on before they cool off.' Lisa gently prodded her mount forward. 'Hiram says your tennis is really good, too. I haven't had a chance for a game with you yet and you've been here a week already. Maybe next week?'

'I'd like that. I know you're busy. Running Palmetto must be quite a job.'

'Harriet's a pretty good housekeeper. I just keep an eye on things. I've been helping Daniel . . . '

'What is it he and you do . . . exactly? Is it to do with the hospital?'

'Oh, no, it's Dan's hobbyhorse . . . best ask him about it. Come on, I'll race you to the lake over there. We're back on plantation territory now.'

She urged her horse into a canter and Lucy followed.

Ask Daniel indeed! Chance'd be a fine thing. Apart from that one abrasive encounter by the pool on her first night she'd caught only fleeting glimpses of him. Lisa had told her he had rooms at the mansion, but rarely used them except when Hiram Senior took a turn for the worse.

Hiram's energy had been revived by Lucy's arrival. He insisted on seeing her every day, sometimes with Clark, to talk about her family, but mostly it was just the two of them.

When Lucy and Lisa returned to the house there was a message: *Mr. Hiram Senior requests the pleasure of Miss Lucy's company — in the movie theatre.*

'Poor you.' Lisa read the note over Lucy's shoulder. 'Dad's favourite subject, after genealogy that is — the history of the Southern states and Palmetto. All on film — we've seen it lots of times. You'll be a brand new audience.'

'I'm interested — really. I know hardly anything about American history.'

'Aw . . . don't tell that to Dad. We'll never see you again. If you're not out of there by supper time we'll send in the cavalry.'

'Thanks. I'll shower and then go down. This is all new to me, Lisa. I love it.'

The movie theatre had been converted from underground garages in the 1960s when films were Hiram's passion. Lucy had seen it on her first tour of the mansion but had never seen it in action. As she went down the steps into the basement she could hear the sounds of gunfire, roaring planes, exploding bombs, all orchestrated by deafening music. She went straight in.

The cinema could seat around one hundred people. Hiram was in splendid isolation centre-aisle, in his wheelchair, absorbed in a black-and-white war film.

'Mr Bojangle.' Lucy touched his shoulder.

'What . . . ah . . . Lucy. Hold it.' He pressed the remote control button and the noise abruptly ceased. 'Fine film that — 'Sergeant York.' You seen it?'

Lucy shook her head.

'You must. I'll arrange it one evening. A family film show, like we used to in the old days.'

'That'd be nice. How are you today?'

'Fine . . . fine. I don't want to talk about my health — I have enough of that up there. Just change that film over. This is what I want to show you. Everyone treating you all right?'

'Of course, Mr Bojangle.'

'Call me Hiram, Lucy. All this English formality . . . Not that I don't admire you folk from the UK. It's just . . . well . . . Mr Bojangle! I'm family, Lucy. Got it?'

'Yes . . . Hiram. I've got it.'

'Good. Now we can get down to business. I wanna show you all about Palmetto. Wasn't always like this. Video's over there, left of the screen . . .'

The first images were scratchy, monochrome stills: the antebellum mansion at the turn of the century was solid, well built and well-kept. Hiram then fast-forwarded for some time.

'Aah, here we are. Now — how about that?'

'That's not Palmetto is it?' Lucy was surprised.

'Yup.' He was pleased by her surprise. 'Pretty run down, ain't it?'

It was difficult to believe it was the same plantation. The camera panned over dilapidated outhouses, broken-paned conservatories, unkempt gardens and exhausted fields covered in weeds.

'It's terrible,' Lucy gasped. 'Whatever happened? Even the house looks about to go to rack and ruin. It's just awful.'

'Damned well was. I took those pictures when I got back from overseas. Three years fighting for the US of A, and when I came back — I'm facing ruin! It was the managers I left in charge that did it. Moved their families in and ran the place down. I soon got rid of them though.'

'Hiram, that's just terrible. How did you manage to sort it out again?'

'Worked twenty four hours a day . . . acted ruthless . . . lost two wives. Both left me, couldn't stand the loneliness. Then God sent me Ellie — my reward and a last chance. Four sons and a daughter. I'm lucky. Palmetto began to make big profits. Expanded the cotton, went into pecan nuts, then in property — that was the best, especially now, and I sure as hell picked the right managers this time.'

'The boys?'

Hiram's snort was dismissive.

'The boys do a good PR job — front men for Bojangle Incorporated. The real work's done in Atlanta and New York City by men who work twelve hours a day plus, if needs be. Oh, don't you worry. I pay 'em well but they sure earn their money . . . ' He tailed off, his head slumped forward.

'Hiram, are you all right? I don't want to tire you . . . '

He stared up, shook his head, stared at her blankly, his colour high.

'Shall I fetch one of the nurses?'

'I'm all right. I wanted to show you . . . it's going to stay that way now . . . ' His voice sank to a mumble and his breath was laboured.

Lucy pressed the panic-button he wore round his neck and a few moments later a couple of nurses came running.

'What's the matter . . . Mr Hiram?' Nurse Paula looked accusingly at Lucy. 'Have you been tiring him?'

''Course she ain't, you fool.' Hiram suddenly came to life again. 'But you may as well take me back now you're here. Lucy, we'll see some more soon and you make sure you come up to say goodnight. I wanna hear about your day . . . '

Lucy put out the lights and went up to her room. The turquoise waters of the pool beckoned her invitingly. There was no one in the water so she was safe from the abrasive Daniel. And there was tennis coaching later with Hiram Junior.

'Not a bad old life,' she told her reflection as she changed yet again, this time from cotton dress to swimsuit.

At the end of her third week at Palmetto, Lucy felt the first twinge of restlessness. The days were always packed, and in the evenings there were plenty of barbecues and dinner parties, either at homes or restaurants. Everyone wanted to meet Lucy and she had more invitations than she could handle.

Hiram Junior, Scott and Corey, vied for her attention but it was Hiram who pressured her most, constantly wanting to be alone with her. So far she'd been able to stall him, often escaping to sit with his father in the top-floor suite.

Occasionally her visits to Hiram Senior would coincide with Daniel's, but he was so coolly aloof she did her best to avoid him. Before she left Palmetto she'd have it out with him, find out what his hang-up was about her visit.

It was a wonderful, fascinating vacation, but she knew it had to end sometime. Impossible to idle away the days, cocooned in the lap of luxury, without a real purpose. She missed her friends and it was time to move on.

One afternoon, Arnold and Joelle called for her and swept her off on their yacht to cruise Charleston Harbour, see the sights, then anchor off the Isle of Palms for a swim. As the sun went down, crew members served supper on deck and Arnold opened champagne.

'Hope you don't mind this spell with the old folks, Lucy — hard to catch you on your own. Joelle tells me you're always hedged in by the Bojangles, especially those boys.'

'Well, they're pretty good hosts — excluding Daniel though.'

'Daniel's a different kettle of Bojangle. Has been since . . . when Joelle?'

'Since Ellie died — there's nothing

wrong with Dan, he's just different. But we want to talk about you, Lucy, not the Bojangle clan. Are you happy here? Nothing worrying you? You . . . you spend a lot of time with the old man.'

'He's a love.' Pushing a crisp into a spicy dip, Lucy missed the wry glance that passed between Joelle and Arnold. 'He knows so much about the American Civil War and all that happened here, I could listen to him for hours — and who wouldn't be happy . . . all this . . . ' She gestured around the luxury yacht and towards the ocean, tinged faintly silver by the rising moon. 'But of course, though it's been the most fabulous holiday, I've got to go home soon.'

Arnold poured sparkling wine into tall, fluted crystal.

'Do you have to go back to Stonebridge? Seemed to me you had a bad deal there . . . apart from your delightful cottage, of course.'

'I know I'm going to miss everyone — especially you two.' Lucy sipped the wine that Arnold had handed her.

'We'd like you to stay for ever, but Stonebridge is Lucy's home, Arnold. She can't just quit it,' Joelle said, serving out Southern fried chicken.

'Don't see why not — new home and family over here — tailor-made.'

'It has to be Lucy's choice. Has anyone put any . . . pressure on you to stay on?' Joelle chose her words carefully. Much as she loved all the Bojangle family she didn't entirely trust Hiram Senior. There was usually a dubious motive somewhere where he was concerned.

'No — not exactly, though Mr Bojangle does get agitated if I broach the subject of leaving, and I don't want to upset him. His health . . . '

'Hiram's a toughie — don't you worry. It's just . . . Arnold and I'll be away for a while and I want to make sure you're all right. We have to go to New York soon to see the family. Toby's graduating and we'd sure like to attend the ceremony.'

'Of course. Toby's your grandson? When is it?'

'A couple of weeks time.'

'I'll have left Palmetto by then. I've been here nearly a month already.'

'I've got a great idea,' Arnold said enthusiastically. 'Why not come with us?'

'Oh, yes do!' Joelle clapped her hands. 'Lisa's coming, too. She and Toby are . . . well, pretty keen on each other. They're only waiting for him to finish law school to get engaged. We can all show you New York. Do say yes, Lucy, it'd be such fun for you to meet Herbert and Annie an' all.'

'I shouldn't really stay at Palmetto much longer . . . two weeks . . . '

'We could leave earlier. Drive up — see some more of the USA.'

'I'd like that, if you're sure.'

'Certainly are. I'll call on Hiram tomorrow.'

Arnold topped up their glasses.

'Let's drink to that — Lucy's New York adventure.'

They all clinked glasses and Lucy felt happier than she had been for a long time. Arnold and Joelle were like parents to her.

* * *

It wasn't too late when Lucy got back to go up and say goodnight to Hiram Senior, but the housekeeper met her at the door, face creased with worry.

'Lucy, I shouldn't go up tonight. Mr Bojangle's not too well. I called the consultant, and Dan's with him. They're settling him for the night.

'What happened? Not a stroke?' The old man clung to life with his finger tips. Another stroke could dislodge him altogether.

'No, nothing like that. It's just . . . something's happened in the family which has upset him. Just so long as he keeps calm — a good night's sleep, Daniel says.'

'Of course I won't disturb him. I just hope he'll be all right.'

'Lucy! Where've you been?' Hiram Junior ran down the central staircase, looking unusually dishevelled and distraught.

'Out on the boat with Joelle and Arnold. They invited me.'

'Gee, Lucy, I wish you'd been here. I sure need someone to talk to right now. Come outside a while.'

'I'm a bit tired, Hiram. I was just going to bed. I'm sorry about your father.'

'Aw, he'll be all right. He's just hopping mad. Blood pressure rocketing according to Dan.' He grabbed her hand. 'Please, Lucy, I need to get out of here.'

'I . . . ' But her protests went unheeded as Hiram pulled her out of the house. 'Where . . . ?'

'Doesn't matter where. I just need a walk.'

'Hiram, do tell me what's happened.' She stopped and shook her hand free. 'Otherwise I don't move another step.'

He looked down at her, ran his hands

through his hair — in the darkness she could just make out a strange expression in his eyes, intense, glittering. Suddenly he bent down, put his hands round her waist and lifted her to him.

'Hiram,' she gasped, 'put me down. What's the matter with you?'

For several seconds he held her, and the more she twisted and turned the firmer he pinned her to him. His lips just touched her throat briefly, then he lowered her to her feet, still holding her loosely but away from him, and though he continued staring at her, his eyes were more normally focused.

'Pardon me, Lucy. I'm . . . sorry. Today's been one hell of a day.'

They both turned as a crunch of gravel warned of someone coming.

'Hiram — what are you doing out here?' Daniel's tall figure loomed out of the darkness and Lucy broke away from Hiram as Daniel came up to them. 'Well, well,' he drawled, 'it's Miss Lucy out here, too. Kinda ubiquitous around here, aren't you?'

'I'm visiting here, remember? Do you want me to stay in my room all day?'

He turned away from her and spoke to his brother.

'There was no call to hare off like that. Dad's calmed down — accepted the inevitable. You know how he feels about ex-wives, but he doesn't blame you for what Hilde's done.'

'Double-dyed stupid bitch,' Hiram swore violently. 'Pardon me, Lucy. Hilde's my first wife. Damn truck-load of trouble. Always was.'

'What's happened that's upset your father so much?'

'We should go in now,' Daniel interrupted. 'It'll be common knowledge tomorrow. Scott and Corey phoned. I told them to stay over in Savannah. I'll sleep here tonight — just in case Dad doesn't settle.'

They walked back to the house in silence, Lucy noting it was the younger man whose arm was thrown protectively around his older brother's shoulder. For all their differences, they appeared united in worry over their father. A pang of loneliness hit her very hard and she longed for her cottage. It'd be good to be back there, safe and familiar behind its heavy, oak door.

Maybe she'd ring the airport tomorrow for flight times home. Much as she loved Arnold and Joelle, she didn't know whether she could cope with another happy united family — the New York Rastes! The comparison was still poignant.

As they went up the front steps a wind sprang up. Warm, humid air swept across the tree tops and she felt her hair whipping her face. As she tossed it back Daniel said casually, 'A summer storm's brewing. Hurricane season's starting!'

6

The story broke next day. The Bojangle dynasty was always newsworthy on account of its wealth and diverse business interests, and the marriage/divorce saga of Hiram Senior and his three eldest sons was always salacious reading. Between them they'd clocked up nine weddings, ranging from the first-time grand church extravaganza to discreet civil ceremonies.

The latest catastrophe which had plunged Palmetto into turmoil was the news that Hilde Bojangle, Hiram Junior's first wife, had used her father-in-law's forged signature for collateral to raise huge loans to set up a business in Australia. The business had gone bankrupt, the loans called in, and Hiram billed for the debt.

He had to decide whether to fight it through the courts and drop more dollars into the bottomless black hole of legal pockets or pay up and write off the debt. The whole unsavoury incident tipped the balance towards implementing a plan he'd been thinking about ever since Lucy had arrived at Palmetto. Around midday he sent for her to join him for lunch in his suite.

Subdued by the previous night's encounter with Hiram Junior, Lucy was wary. She'd slept badly, the weather had turned sultry and very humid. It was unpleasant outside, unnaturally air-conditioned inside.

Hiram watched her closely.

'Eat up, don't pick at your food. I thought you liked cajun chicken. You're looking pale today. Something upset you — someone not treat you right?'

'No, everyone's very kind. I had a lovely day out yesterday with Joelle and Arnold out on their boat. It's just a bit hot,' she finished tamely.

'Have some blueberry pie then — with mango ice cream. Bet you can't resist that, eh?' He fussed and flapped over her from his wheelchair.

'You spoil me. You've got to know my weak spots. I'm a pig for ice cream.'

'That's better. Have some more.' Nurse Paula came in with coffee. 'Put it down — and, Paula, make yourself scarce. I wanna talk to Lucy in private.'

'You shouldn't tire yourself, not after yesterday. Daniel said you need all the rest you can get.'

'Rest! You'll all have me resting into my grave before long. I'm OK — OK?'

'If you say so . . . sir.' Paula gave Lucy a cool nod and left them.

'I sure do,' Hiram called after her. 'OK, Lucy, I want to talk to you — real serious now. Drink up your coffee and listen. You've told me a deal about your family farm in England. I know it meant a lot to you, and I've told you I'm real sorry about what happened. But that's over now — in the past.

'Present and future, that's what you young 'uns should be concerned with. I don't have a future now — not much of a present come to think, but I gotta

102

secure the past for your futures. That makes sense, girl?'

'Yes, but it's not really my future, it's your family's — your sons, and Lisa's.'

'We're getting there, Lucy. You know Clark's been working real hard tracing your family line? So far he's established a slim connection. British Beaujangles left Plymouth, Devonshire, in the late 1600s. Your ancestors. Mine, too. He's certain of that — we're from the same stock. Think of that Lucy. All Bojangles. Same blood, but distant enough for . . . ' He stopped abruptly.

'Distant enough for what?' The mango ice cream slid deliciously down her throat. She'd miss all this pampering, being spoiled, waited on, the wonderful food. TV dinners in Stonebridge would be pretty lack-lustre by comparison.

Hiram changed tack suddenly, ignoring her interruption.

'Your mother and father — were they happily married? How long? To each other all the time? No side-steps in between?'

Lucy put down her spoon in astonishment. The thought of either parent side-stepping, as Hiram quaintly put it, was ludicrous.

'Of course to each other. Clark's got all the records. Nearly forty years. We were . . . planning a surprise party, Matt and I.' She faltered, blinked, and went on firmly. 'Yes, Hiram, they were very happy . . . always. Dad must have suffered dreadfully, keeping all the burden to himself.

'It was because he loved Mum and us . . . he didn't want to hurt us. Anyway, their marriage was rock-solid, same as my gran's and grandad's — married fifty years. Never a day apart apparently — died within a week of each other.'

'Aah.' The old man's sigh was poignant. 'What a background! Gee, that's mighty unusual — especially round here!' He was silent for some time contemplating the novelty of one marriage per couple, per lifetime.

''Course . . . if I'd met Ellie right away . . . ' He sighed again. 'But maybe not. I just couldn't fit wives into rebuilding Palmetto. Sometimes life just ain't very fair.'

Lucy refrained from commenting that Hiram Senior hadn't done too badly.

'And what about you, Lucy? What's your view on marriage? Arnold told me about your fiancé . . . needs to see a shrink, passing up a girl like you.'

Lucy put down her coffee cup carefully and thought awhile.

'Come on, no need to be shy with me.' Hiram moved his chair closer to her.

'I'm not shy. It's just that after Pete I've not thought . . . it's too soon. But of course I'd like to marry some time, have a family . . . '

'Good girl, good girl. No sense letting the past sour up the present. You've a new home and a new family now. Fresh start. Just settle down at Palmetto, pick out a suite of rooms, redecorate . . . refurnish to your taste. Soon tidy up your affairs in England. Best if Arnold goes over . . . maybe with Joelle.'

'Hiram! Hang on. What are you talking about? I never intended to stay here for ever. I've just loved this holiday and I'd like to visit again. I've grown fond of everyone. But I live in Devon. My home's there.'

'What home? Oh, yeah, I've seen Arnold's video of your little cottage. Kinda cute. Keep it as a holiday place if you want. That's no problem at all — but you've no job, no money. I'm offering you a real home here with us. You won't need to work again. Tell you what.' He grasped the arm of his chair with his good hand. 'I've one terrific idea. Why don't we write up the history of the Palmetto together? Clark'll help with research. A kinda documentary. Hey, it could be a film, too!'

'Hiram — stop! Please.' It was incredible enough to be almost laughable. The old man was vibrant with plans for her future — his plans for her future! He was so animated the years had rolled off him. She saw the young man again, planning, scheming, and Lucy saw with sorrow that Hiram Senior would never last long as an invalid. He needed action to keep him alive.

'Hiram, I'm truly grateful for what you've given me. Being at Palmetto has been such an experience — it's opened my eyes to lots of things, but it's time to go home now. I feel so much better — I can put the tragedy behind me and start again. And it's been you, and Arnold, I have to thank for that . . . '

'No! You can't go. Not yet. I'll give you anything you want. You've got to stay. You must . . . ' He was interrupted by the ringing of his telephone. 'Darn it. Bojangle Senior . . . oh, Arnold. OK, yes, surely. Right now I'm with Lucy. See you in a minute then.'

Nurse Paula put her head round the door as he clicked off the phone.

'Mr Hiram, it's time for your rest.

Daniel'll raise a riot . . . '

'All right. Just a word with Arnold Raste. He's on his way. Lucy, promise me you won't do anything hasty. We'll talk again. Promise now.'

'All right, I promise — for the moment, but I am going home, Hiram — and soon.' Impulsively she bent and kissed his cheek. 'You've been so good to me. I'm so grateful.'

'Umph. Go along then. What you doing now?'

'Hiram fixed a coaching session for the afternoon, but I'm not so sure.'

She was reluctant to face him after last night. Maybe Lisa would go with her.

'Do you good. You're a mite pale today. Come and see me this evening.'

Lucy passed Arnold B. Raste on the stairs to Hiram's suite.

'Hi, Lucy, hear you had lunch with Hiram. Did you tell him about New York?'

'No, I didn't get the chance.'

'Shall I? Joelle's real set on it.

Telephoned Herbert and Annie last night and they're just thrilled. Can't wait to meet you.'

'Hiram's being . . . a bit difficult about me leaving at all. I'll be glad if you would mention it, Arnold. Make it seem more certain. I have to go back to England.'

''Course you do, my dear Lucy. I'll handle Hiram . . . leastways I'll try. You go and enjoy yourself.'

But what Hiram Bojangle III had to say to his attorney chased all thoughts of that New York trip out of his mind. He'd assumed, when Hiram sent for him, it was the Hilde affair he'd wanted to discuss, but that was dismissed right away.

'Can't be helped. Just goes to show what fool choices of wives those sons of mine make. Like father, like son, I suppose. There'll be no Bojangle dollars left to inherit at this rate. Once the guys in Atlanta have assessed the damage they'll be in touch with you folk — settle up — no long court case.'

Nurse Paula came in with a tray.

'Time for your medication, sir.'

He waved her away.

'Stop worrying me woman . . . ' he snapped moodily.

'Hiram . . . Paula's got a job to do.' Arnold placated the girl with a smile.

'I know. Pardon me, Paula. Just ten minutes with Arnold here then I promise I'll be a model patient. Now scat. Ten minutes.' She disappeared.

'OK, Arnold. Don't interrupt. I've got nine and a half minutes before Florence Nightingale comes back, and I won't be able to stall her next time. Sit down. Pour yourself a stiff drink.'

'Bit early, but I'll take coffee, please.'

'You know where it is. Help yourself.'

He waited until Arnold was seated with his coffee.

'Arnold, do you think Lucy'd be interested in one of my boys?'

'Interested? In what way?'

'There's only one way. Don't be a dope. They all seem keen. Hiram's a front-runner so far, but Scott and

110

Corey aren't so slow. I see it all, Arnold — from up here — I've got my spies. Just think — British blood — and a Bojangle! Family background of good, solid marriages — they don't enter into it lightly.

'All my work at Palmetto, leeched away by those damned ex-wife bimbos, and once I'm gone, they'll be doing the same thing all over again. Not an ounce of horse sense between the lot of 'em.'

'Hiram, don't get excited, it can't be good for you. What foolish notion's in your head now? Lucy's been badly hurt by one man and I doubt she's ready to be thrust in the arms of another to suit your convenience. Don't play with fire. Could be some people'll be badly burned.'

'When I want your advice on family matters I'll ask for it. I'm being straight with you now because we're old friends and you've been my attorney a long time. Better take some more coffee — and take it black,' he announced, mock-casual. 'I'm changing my lawyer, Arnold.'

Arnold was shocked but wasn't going to let it show. He was used to Hiram's games and was pretty good at keeping at least a move ahead. But this one was a puzzle, and worse, he was afraid it had to do with Lucy. Equally casually, he replied, 'Found a cheaper firm, Hiram? I'm not prepared to do deals. We've got along pretty well over all these years . . . '

'Ain't you going to show just a little emotion? Crack the façade a mite . . . be a bit stirred . . . just to please me?'

'You're an old devil. OK, I'll admit it. I'm a bit shaken. Are you going to tell me why?'

'You'll thank me for it. I'm going to do something you won't approve of so I'm letting you off the hook by employing someone else.' He relented. 'Don't worry, you're keeping most of the Bojangle business. You're the best firm of corporate attorneys I know.

That's your field. I need a specialist in inheritance law. I'm altering my will, Arnold, that's all.'

Relief and terror mixed equally in Arnold's brain. He tried to keep cool.

'All right, Hiram, I was pretty shaken at first. I thought you were pulling the whole carpet from under — but it's just a little rug. We can deal with your will. You've tinkered about with it often enough . . . codicils . . . bequests . . . '

'This is different. I need to tie things up real tight.'

'Won't you tell me, as a friend, what you're proposing?'

'You don't catch me like that — I wasn't born yesterday, you know that. You'd only wear me out trying to make me change my mind — and I ain't going to. I'm going to fix Palmetto's future. It won't be going to rack and ruin again.'

'We can tie that up. There are trusts . . . '

'I know that, I'm not crazy.' Hiram banged his stick on the floor. 'This is personal. I'm not saying any more, I'm tired — fetch that nurse in.'

'One question, Hiram. It's not . . . not to do with Lucy is it? You aren't going to . . . '

'Arnold B. Raste, you do think I've gone crazy, don't you? You think I'm so smitten with the English Rose I'm going to leave all my money to her . . . '

'It'd be terrible. She'd spend her life fighting law suits from the family. It wouldn't do, it really wouldn't. It'd ruin her life.'

'Aw hush up, Arnold. I thought you'd more sense. D'you really take me for such a senile, old idiot? I know what I'm going to do and that's the end of it. Thought it only fair to let you know. You'll be hearing from Rudge, Ildowski and Wermter pretty soon. Pass all the documents relating to my will over to them. Now, where's that danged nurse? Paula!'

Nurse Paula came into the room again with her tray of medication, and a strange look on her face. The doors

114

were thick and solid but she'd strained to hear at the keyhole and heard enough to disturb her.

It was in her best interest to report back to Corey Bojangle everything that went on in Hiram Senior's sick-room suite. He'd be very interested and alarmed by what she'd just heard.

'No arguments this time, Mr Hiram. You must take your pills and then have a good, long sleep.'

* * *

'Lisa, wait for me.' Lucy, dressed in tennis gear, ran down the front steps.

'Hi. I hear you're coming to New York with us. That's great. I'd love for you to meet Toby. He's . . . he's an incredible guy.'

'Why've you not mentioned him before?'

'Aw, I'm kinda shy about it. I guess . . . it's early days . . . he was here in the spring. That's when it all happened, but we thought we'd hold back until he graduated. He wants to come back here to practise law. Maybe Arnold's firm. Anyway, it'll be good to have you meet him.'

'Nothing's decided yet, but I'm tempted. Look, can you come with me now? Tennis coaching — it's more fun when you're there. Hiram gets a bit serious when it's just me.'

'Sorry, I can't. I promised Joelle I'd call round to talk about the trip. I don't think Hiram'll be coaching you today — but you should go along to the courts, especially if you like gladiator sports. Hiram and Dan are shooting it out today.'

'Shooting?'

'Sure — on the tennis court. Mean friends my brothers can be. It'll be worth watching. A real killer.'

'Isn't Daniel working?'

'Day off. A rare appearance at Palmetto — but for his match with Hiram everything else can go hang. Even his . . . '

'His what? Just what does he do, Lisa?'

'Ask him. He'll maybe tell you — if he wins. Corey's down there. He'll fill you in about the tournament. See you later. I'm going to be late.'

Lucy felt the tension even before she reached the courts. There was none of the usual banter and bickering repartee that went with an ordinary tennis match. Grim silence was broken only by explosive grunts of effort and the smack of dedicated ball on racket. Neither Daniel nor Hiram acknowledged her, each intent on the game.

'Two match points, Dan,' Corey called from the umpire's chair.

'They need an umpire!' Lucy exclaimed.

'Ssh,' he hissed. 'This is a tournament match.'

'Tournament?' She looked around for more players, or a few spectators.

'Ssh. Quiet please.'

Worse than Wimbledon, she thought, creeping to the nearest seat. The brothers faced each other, bouncing lightly on their feet, rackets twirling, taut as hungry tigers waiting for the kill.

'Dan needs this to equalise,' Corey whispered out of the side of his mouth. 'Don't move a muscle,' he warned.

Daniel threw the ball up to serve and smacked it into court at a low, spinning angle. An ace!

'Advantage, Dan. Match point,' Corey cracked out.

To Lucy they both looked good enough for Wimbledon. In the final gruelling rally, Dan clinched victory with a ferocious, dynamite overhead smash. He vaulted over the net with a victory whoop.

'Evens! Five matches all. Thanks, Hiram.'

'I'll lick you yet. Still five to go. Good game,' Hiram conceded. 'Oh, no, Lucy, I clean forgot our coaching session, and I've a meeting this afternoon in Charleston. How about tomorrow?'

'I'll see.' Lucy was relieved — remembering last night, though

Hiram showed not the least trace of embarrassment. 'It's too hot for me anyway — and that super-charged tennis is really intimidating. I'll have a swim instead.' She saw Corey recording the result, each brother solemnly signing. 'I guess this is serious stuff. Is there a prize at the end?'

'Nope. Just the honour,' Corey explained. 'It's a Bojangle tradition. Ever since us kids could hold a racket. Mom was a real tennis fan — Forest Hills, Wimbledon an' all. She organised a friendly tournament, summer through to fall, for family and friends.

'Toby used to partner Lisa before he moved to New York. Can't recall when it got serious, after Mom died I guess. We have a wing-dinger of a grand finale in the Fall. It's always the same, Hiram and Dan slogging it out in the last match.'

'It's a real big event here.' Hiram sat beside her. 'Marquee, barbecue, dancing, dawn breakfast. You'll love it, Lucy.'

'The Fall. Goodness, I'll be back in England long before the autumn.'

'You're leaving?' Dan slung a towel round his neck and looked directly at her for the first time.

' 'Course she isn't. Hogwash — the old man won't hear of it. Neither will I. We've got you here, and we're going to keep you here.' Hiram pulled on a sweater. 'I gotta go now, but we'll fix a dinner date real soon — just the two of us. Corey, there's Paula. Looks mighty agitated — making a beeline for you. Dan, would you take Lucy for her swim?' He winked. 'Winner's prize. I'll get some cold drinks sent down to the pool.'

'I can take myself for a swim, thanks — and I don't see myself as a prize.'

'Don't argue, I'll meet you there in ten minutes.' Although Dan didn't look too thrilled with his prize, he didn't look as hostile as usual either. Maybe his win had put him in a good mood. He was as relaxed as she'd ever seen him.

'Tell you what, I'll race you ten lengths. I'll be generous and give you a length start.'

'Keep your start,' Lucy bristled. 'I can beat you any day — on equal terms.'

His smile was lazy.

'Can you now? We'll see about that. No longer than ten minutes.'

7

He was at the pool before her, still bouncing on the balls of his feet, but impatiently this time, muscular body raring to go. Lucy began to regret her boast — he looked a formidable opponent.

'Come on, time to make good that threat.' His dark eyes briefly appraised her perfectly proportioned figure and satiny skin, its peach tones tanned gold by the Carolina sun.

'Can't wait.' She came to stand beside him.

'Go!' he yelled, and they dived in simultaneously.

The cool water was a delicious antidote to the sultry closeness of the day. Lucy was fitter than she'd been for a long time. The outdoor active life had toned her body to peak fitness. Invigorated, she increased the pace.

Daniel kept just behind her all the time, calling out the numbers on each turn.

After eight, Lucy began to tire and wasn't surprised to see him flash past her and touch the side before her on nine. She turned for the final length but he grasped her by the waist and lifted her out of the water.

'OK, you win. Great race.'

'I didn't win. There's another length.'

His arms were still around her, his eyes smiling up at her, glittering water drops patterning his face. She found it hard to breathe as he slowly released her to sink back in the pool.

'I said a length start. Be a good winner.' He pulled himself out of the water.

Lucy floated away on her back, eyes closed, hair darkened by the water, a seaweed halo swirling gently round her head and shoulders. It was peaceful and relaxing, the air thick and warm. Storing up memories against an English winter, she turned and lazily struck out for the steps.

A table was set under a shaded awning with fresh fruit, cool drinks, tortilla chips and savoury dips of hot salsa and cool guacamole. They lay either side of the table on padded loungers.

Daniel broke the silence.

'You're a good swimmer.' Lucy didn't reply, merely stretching out her toes to dry. 'Hiram says your tennis is coming along, too.'

She leaned back on the lounger and slipped on a pair of sunglasses.

'You don't have to make conversation with me. I'm sure that's not part of the prize.'

'What's biting you? I'm not making conversation. Just being friendly.'

'I've been here nearly a month, and today's the first time you've addressed a half-civil word to me. You don't like me being here at all. Your face — when I said I was leaving said it all.' Damn it, what was the matter with her? These were her private thoughts — supposed to be kept inside her head. It was all

Daniel's fault. He made her nervous, and the thoughts had popped into words before she could prevent them.

'I'm sorry,' she muttered. 'Must be the heat. I'm not used to the . . . humidity.'

He didn't say anything for a while, but she felt his eyes on her, knew he was making a thorough examination this time. The give-away blush was spreading to her neck. She reached blindly for a towel.

'Here.' He put one into her hand. 'Need a sun hat, too?'

She got up, shook back her hair and pushed her sunglasses on to her forehead. Might as well finish what she'd started — too late to back track.

'I'm fine thanks. Sorry — again. That was rude of me, but all your family have been so welcoming and kind. I wondered why . . . whether I'd done anything to offend you . . . or whether . . . Hey!' She stopped as Daniel got up, ran to the spring board and dived into the pool.

He broke the surface, gasped for air, then swam back towards her.

'OK.' He flopped back on the lounger. 'Let's start again — from zero. Why did you come here in the first place?'

'You know why. You must do. Because your father wanted to find some English connections. Arnold found me, and Hiram invited me here. Nothing sinister. No ulterior motives. What could there be?'

'I can't guess.'

'Also,' she went on defiantly, 'life was pretty rotten when Arnold turned up in my front garden in June. He was very helpful to me at that time, and then very persuasive. I felt I owed it to him. I didn't see any harm. I still can't, although there's something bugging you about it. Either that or . . . you can't stand the sight of me. Why can't you be straight with me? What makes you so different from the rest of the family? And what do you do that they disapprove of so strongly, when you're

126

not playing the ministering angel to the sick?'

Daniel spread his hands behind his head and laughed.

'My, my, just a tiny touch of sarcasm along with a shower of questions from the cool English Bojangle. Which question do you want me to answer first?'

'I want to know why you hate me being here.'

'I don't. Next.'

'That's not good enough. You've been hostile all the time.'

'Am I hostile now?'

'No . . . but . . . '

'Well then. Guess I'll take the fifth amendment on that one. Anything else?'

'I . . . oh, this isn't what I meant. It's none of my business. I'll go in. You're playing games.'

'Honest, I'm not.' He raised his hands. 'Don't go in — we've hardly started yet. Guess I find it tough to figure you out. Let's even the game up

— if that's what you think it is.
Question for question. Do we have a
deal?'

Perched on the edge of her seat,
ready for flight, Lucy regarded him
suspiciously. Why was he being Mr Nice
Guy today? He looked really interested
in her, and she had to admit he was
even more attractive when he looked
straight into her eyes — like now. She
swallowed.

'A deal then. Your turn, though I
think you evaded my question.'

'OK, straight bat from now on. How
do you like life at Palmetto?'

'That's easy. It's great. I've never
experienced anything like it. A dream
world from the movies. But . . . can I be
really honest?'

'That's the deal.'

'Well, it is a dream world. It's not
real. Not to me. It's a privileged world,
an élite. I feel kind of guilty almost
— being here. Great for a vacation, but
it's time I started work. At least,' she
gave an apologetic laugh, 'look for

128

work. That's a full time career in itself nowadays — especially where I live.'

She had Dan's full attention, leaning forward, watching her closely.

'Your 'real' world? Is that England? Your cute cottage, pretty scenery?'

'Have you ever been to England?'

'Wimbledon, with Mom when I was a kid — but I read the brochures.' He was silent for a few minutes then appeared to have made a decision and stood up abruptly. 'Come on.' He held out his hand. 'We'll take a look at my 'real world'. You're pretty isolated here . . . '

'I've been outside. I know what the real world's like here.'

'Historic Charleston? The slave market? Fine places, but for tourists. I'll give you my tour. Show you the neighbourhood — to get Palmetto Plantation into perspective — and Lucy . . . ' He pulled her to her feet and drew her nearer to him, his grip strong on her wrist. ' . . . don't be under any illusion. My hostility

. . . wasn't because I couldn't stand the sight of you. Just the opposite, I guess. See you in a few minutes. I'll pick you up by the front entrance.'

Once on their way, Daniel turned off the main road and bumped the pick-up truck along an unmetalled road for about a mile. Timber sheeting rattled in the back. Poor-looking, shanty-type dwellings were set back among tall pines, broken-down rockers tilted on sagging porches. Nothing could be a greater contrast to the manicured gardens and well-tended fields of Palmetto.

They turned into a clearing and Lucy gasped in astonishment.

'It's a building site!'

'Yup.' He leaned across and opened her door, his arm warm on her body. 'Hop out and take a look while I unload this timber.'

About a dozen wood-framed, one-storey houses in various stages of completion were set in a semi-circle in the cleared portion of forest. The place

130

hummed with activity, chain saws roaring in the background, felling more trees.

As Lucy took it all in, a young woman jumped down from a ladder and ran to Dan.

'You're here! I was scared you weren't going to make it.' She flung herself into his arms and kissed him, long black hair whirling around in excitement. 'Dan, it's finished. Only a bit of painting — do come and see.'

A small child rushed out of one of the houses screaming, 'Uncle Dan, Uncle Dan.' He picked her up and swung her round until she squealed with delighted terror. 'More . . . more . . . '

He put her down carefully.

'Not now — we've got company. Lucy Beaujangle — from England.'

'England? What's that?'

'It's a tiny island — across the Atlantic Ocean, Chloe.' The woman smiled and held out her hand to Lucy.

'Hi, I'm Megan. You a relative of Dan's?'

'Sort of.' Lucy wasn't too happy with the description of her homeland, but the girl's smile was warm and friendly.

'Dan's brought you to see the project?'

'I guess. What is it exactly?'

'Never heard of Habitat for Humanity? Houses for the homeless — all built with voluntary labour. All this — it's Dan's doing.'

'Not true. The scheme's been going for some time. I just kicked it along a little in this area. Aren't you going to show us your house, Megan?'

'My house! Can you believe it? Chloe, let's do the honours. Our first visitors.'

Everyone called out greetings as they crossed the clearing, but no one stopped working.

'Most of them are on vacation,' Megan explained to Lucy. 'That woman hammering nails is a lawyer; those two fixing the roof manage fast-food outlets.' She stopped and took Lucy's arm. 'If I hadn't met Dan . . . I had to go to hospital . . . he arranged for Chloe to be looked after and then got me on this project. I can't tell you how grateful I am. Now I've got hope, and somewhere to live safely. I've never had either of those things before.'

The house she showed them would have occupied a tiny corner at Palmetto and then been overlooked, but to Megan and Chloe it was ultimate paradise.

'Look, look, a fridge and a freezer.' Megan danced about opening and closing cupboards, poking into a small closet off the bedroom, stopping to hug Dan every time she passed — which was often! 'Isn't it just the greatest place you ever saw? I have such plans for the yard. A friend's given me a barbecue. Are you coming back tonight, Dan? I could cook supper . . . your cousin, too.'

'No. I'm taking Lucy back now. I'll

maybe stop by again later this evening.' He gave Chloe a hug and kissed Megan.

She clung to him.

'Dan, I just love you — you know that?'

He kissed her again and lifted her hair away from her neck.

'I know that, Megan. Your hair's wet through. Calm down a bit — it's too hot to get so up in the air.'

'I don't care how hot it is — and I never want to come down from this cloud.'

Lucy had a hard job keeping a bright smile on her face. Her stomach felt leaden and she felt dizzy and sick.

'You OK?' Dan took her arm and for a second she swayed against him.

'Yes. It's just so hot.'

'Feeling better?' He turned on the air conditioning in the car. 'So, that's one of your questions answered. I help organise housing schemes for the homeless. Dad and my brothers think it's lunatic — 'do-gooders for no-hopers'!'

'Megan didn't seem a no-hoper.'

'She was once. Single mother, trying to run two lousy-paid jobs — one wage going to child care, no chance ever of housing — '

'Is it free — where she is?'

'God, no. We're in business to make a profit to plough into more housing. We give her a low-cost mortgage. The houses are cheap, the land's donated, most labour's voluntary. If we have the money we can run up a house in a few weeks. They'll not last as long as Palmetto with its solid stone and brick. Palmetto's designed to last down the generations — built on slave labour — naturally!'

'It's all very worthy.' Lucy felt flat, dispirited. The question she really wanted to ask was how he felt about Megan. It was obvious Megan was head-over-heels in love with Dan. Instead, she asked, 'Why? Why do you give so much time and energy? Don't you work hard enough as a doctor?'

'Guess after Mom died, we all went

our different ways. Before that I was a rich, spoiled kid who thought everyone had a swimming pool in the back yard. I couldn't stand Palmetto once Mom had gone. I decided to travel before Medical School . . . you hungry? How about a hamburger? Had one yet?'

'No thanks. We have them on our tiny little island, too. They're not a novelty, and they're extremely bad for you.'

'Didn't take you for a killjoy. Nothing wrong with hamburgers. American food's every bit as good as Arnold's Creole cuisine.'

'And you a doctor!'

'Tell you what, you don't lecture me on diet, and I'll not lecture you on homelessness. I'll get my hamburger when I've dropped you off.'

'Where did you travel? Did you go on your own?'

'Went with Toby, Arnold's grandson. Had a great time at first. Europe — all the high spots except the UK, don't recall why not. Pockets full of money — all the best places. Then something

136

happened that changed me for good. Sure you want to hear this boring old stuff?'

Lucy nodded.

'We got in a fight in a bar. Drunken show-offs — Toby and I and a few guys. Police broke it up, put us in the cells for the night to cool off. I was put in a cell with this back-packer. Tried to murder each other at first — bosom pals by dawn, and I was committed to going to India with him. Toby wasn't too thrilled but he came along.

'In India I saw such grinding poverty, I couldn't believe it. I won't bore you with the details but after that I never could view Palmetto in quite the same light. I realised how privileged I was and I decided I had to give something back, that's all. Now, I'm going to get you back then go for my hamburger.'

In the car, Lucy stole sidelong glances at Dan's profile. He was frowning, concentrating on the increasingly heavy, homeward-bound traffic. Remote, aloof, back in his own world.

Building site or hospital? Not Palmetto, Lucy guessed. At least he'd revealed some of the enigma today.

'Why medicine?' she asked.

'Don't you ever stop? Why don't you think of a career as an investigating journalist? You'd do well as an interviewer. Well, it had to be something different from business. I wasn't going to be a Bojangle front guy. Dad's cute enough to have real dedicated tough guys at the helm of Bojangle Incorporated. The back-pack buddy was a medical student. He talked a lot about it and it seemed a logical choice. Dad stamped his feet a lot, but I convinced him it was a 'vocational call', and that I'd seen the light in India. Didn't really give him a choice — upped sticks and left. And that's enough. I'm mighty tired of all this. Fortunately, here we are at Palmetto.'

'But where do you live? And why?'

He stopped the car, turned to face her, and for a long moment there was silence. Lucy was sure he must hear her

138

heart thumping, but without taking his eyes off hers, he said softly, 'No more questions, cousin Lucy. Understand?'

Then slowly he brought his mouth to hers, lingered, exerted the subtlest of sweet pressure, and released her.

As he did so a car screeched to a stop alongside them. The driver's window slid down and Hiram Junior yelled out, 'What on earth are you playing at, Daniel?'

Before Dan had time to respond, the front door was flung open and Lisa ran down the front steps followed by a grave-faced Arnold Raste.

In a second, Dan was running towards them.

'What's happened? Dad?'

'No, no, it's Toby. He's had an accident on his motor bike. He's in hospital. I've got to go to New York with Joelle and Arnold. They've come to collect me. Dan, he will be all right, won't he?'

Dan put his arm round his sister.

'Toby's a tough guy. How serious is it?'

Lisa turned to Arnold.

'We don't know yet. He's unconscious. They can't be sure how bad the damage is. That's why we've got to go, tonight.'

'Sure. And I'll get on to the hospital right away — see if I can get any more information. Do you want me to come with you?'

'No.' Arnold shook his head. 'Later maybe, when we see what the situation is. OK to phone you from the airport? You might have gleaned some news by then. They were mighty cagey with me. It's worrying.'

'Not necessarily so. They'll need to run tests.'

Hiram tried to detain Lucy as she got out of the car.

'You been out with Dan all day?'

She shook off his arm.

'Hiram, can't you see, something's happened. Lisa and Arnold are upset. And if I have been out with Dan all day,

I don't see that it's any of your business.'

'You don't? Well, I disagree. It's time you and I did some straight talking. How about that dinner date? Tonight?'

'I must talk to Lisa. I don't think tonight's appropriate in the circumstances.'

'Tomorrow for certain then?'

'Oh, Hiram! I don't know. Let's sort this out first.'

She ran up the steps and into the house.

Hiram watched her go, his face a study of mutinous, frustrated fury.

'Lucy Beaujangle,' he muttered as he stormed into his car, 'you are heading for a whole heap of trouble.'

8

So, you guys gotta do something about this very serious situation.' Corey shot the numbered ball neatly into the pocket and swiftly followed it by potting the black. 'My game — I win. Want another?'

'Now,' Scott flung himself into a deep leather sofa and put his feet up, 'we need an action plan. Who'da thought it? The old man's finally gone senile.'

'You've no evidence of that.' Hiram replaced his cue on the rack, walked over to the bar at the other end of the pool room and brought out three beers from the fridge. He tossed one to each brother. 'And no doctor would back you up. Dad's in sound mind and there's nothing to stop him from changing his will.'

'Whose side are you on?' Corey took a deep drink of his beer.

'Ours, of course. I just don't think we should act too hasty until we know what it is he's going to do.'

'What exactly did Paula hear?' Scott sat down beside Corey.

'She couldn't hear it all — I told you. But Dad's getting a new lawyer and changing his will. Paula distinctly heard the old man say ' . . . the English Rose. I'm going to leave it all to her.' '

'He couldn't! Dad's too family-minded.'

'He's convinced she is family, and you know his obsession about our ex-wives. He's convinced as soon as he's dead we'll all remarry and get divorced again — and bingo, whacks of Bojangle dollars sucked into alimony payments. His life work squandered.' Hiram fetched three more beers.

'I don't intend to remain celibate the rest of my life,' Scott grumbled. 'Carol's getting real mean with me 'cos I won't come up with the goods.'

'Exactly!' Corey sat up. 'That's just what the old man's scared of, and it's not unprecedented. Courts are littered with contested law suits — senile, old guys doing dotty things, cutting out their families.'

'Who's the new lawyer? Paula pick that up?'

'Yeah, just about. Rudge, Ilklow something and Wermter.'

'Bulls-eye!' Hiram smashed his fist into his palm. 'No problem. Henry Wermter's at the sailing club most weekends, and he owes me a favour. I'll get him to nose around, find out exactly what the old man's intentions are. Then we can make a move. Another game anyone?'

'Can't.' Corey got up. 'I promised Paula I'd take her into town.'

'And I'm seeing Carol.' Scott put on his jacket.

'That leaves the field clear for you, Hiram — and the English Rose! Though I hear she was out with Dan all day.'

'Yeah. He took her to that crazy project — Environment something or other. I wouldn't call that an important date. He's a fool, thank goodness. I'll ring Henry Wermter right now, get the ball rolling. See you guys.'

* * *

Of all the opulent splendour and luxury of Palmetto, Lucy would miss the pool most of all. She loved it, especially as now when there was no one else in it. She swam ten fast work-out lengths then a leisurely and infinitely pleasurable five more. A violent thunderstorm in the night had kept her awake, but it had cleared the humidity and freshened the air.

It was a perfect morning: azure sky, wonderful dry heat and the coolest of zephyr breezes. Wonderful. Blissful. She turned on her back. One more length and she'd get out and think what to do with the rest of her life!

She sneaked another two before climbing out. Stretching out on the lounger was equal bliss. If ever she won the lottery . . . a modest house, huge swimming pool, donation to Daniel's project . . . She tensed. That was the problem!

Every time she started to re-plan her life or think about leaving Palmetto, Daniel's broad-shouldered body and dark, expressive eyes loomed into her head. She couldn't help thinking about what he'd told her.

What had happened in India? Why did he get into the fight in the bar? She kept seeing him with Megan in his arms, Chloe holding his hand, looking like a family unit. Were they? Where did he live? She didn't even know that.

'Oh, stop it!' she shouted out, holding her head.

A shadow fell across her chair, blocking the sun.

'Pardon me, ma'am.' One of the house servants carrying a tray with champagne in an ice-bucket and two fluted glasses bent to place it beside her. 'Mr Hiram Senior's compliments, Miss Lucy.'

146

Lucy looked up and saw the old man propelling his wheelchair across the terrace, a male nurse following at a discreet distance.

'Fine morning, Lucy. Mind if I join you? Storm disturb you last night?'

'A little, but I've had a marvellous swim. I feel fine. Any news of Toby?'

'Dan's phoning right now. I hope you'll take a glass of champagne with me.'

'It's a bit early . . .'

'Special day. We always used to have champagne. Ellie's favourite. Wedding anniversary — would have been thirty-five years.'

'In that case, thank you, I will.'

Once the wine was poured, Hiram waved away his attendants.

'Makes me feel so helpless, all this fussing! Lucy here'll see me back upstairs. It's so good to be out of that damned sick-room!' He raised his glass. 'Here's to Ellie Bojangle — my dear wife. You'd have loved her, Lucy.'

'I'm sure I would.'

'If only she'd been alive she'd've seen to it these danged sons of ours picked better wives. Never be in this mess.' He looked at her shrewdly. 'How you getting along with them? Good-looking boys, aren't they? Can't deny that. I believe Hiram's looking for you.' But it was Dan who came on to the terrace to join them five minutes later. 'Champagne, Dan?' Hiram asked.

'No thanks, I'm working. Due at the hospital right now. Thought I'd let you know there's no change in Toby. He's still unconscious. I'll maybe fly over at the weekend. See you.' With the briefest of nods to Lucy he was gone and somehow, for Lucy, the morning had lost its sparkle.

'Can't fathom that boy at all.' Hiram shook his head. 'Cuckoo in the nest. Don't seem to want to live like the rest of us. Won't settle here, has an apartment in town near the hospital. Danged if I understand him. This one now ... Hiram Junior, he's a pretty straight-forward sorta guy. He'll join us in a glass I'll bet.'

'Sure will, but it's Lucy I want — to make sure of our dinner date tonight.'

'I didn't agree to . . . '

'You two planning a date?' Hiram Senior held his glass out for more wine. 'You bet I'll drink to that. Take her to the Flamingo Grill, son — smartest place in town. Best of everything. I'll telephone . . . '

'No need, Dad, I've already fixed it.'

'But I didn't say I'd go,' Lucy protested.

'But you will,' Hiram Senior said urgently, 'you will. To please me — and Ellie. It's our anniversary, remember.'

The younger man put his hand on Lucy's shoulder.

'No question, Dad. Not a reason in the world not to. We'll have a great time. Pick you up at half-past six, Lucy. Gotta dash now — some clients to fly up to Myrtle Beach.' And he was gone, before Lucy could open her mouth to protest.

Hiram Senior slapped his good hand

up and down on the chair arm.

'Great, made my day. Hiram'll show you a real good time. You make sure you tell me all about it tomorrow.' He yawned widely. 'Guess I'll have to go sleep off the champagne. But it's done me the power of good. I knew Ellie'd fix it.'

Perhaps he is beginning to lose touch with reality, Lucy thought as she wheeled him across the terrace. The wine had made her sleepy, too, and the soft bed of her sumptuous suite was the only place she wanted to be. She'd worry about dinner with Hiram Junior later. Plenty of time yet.

She wished Lisa was still around. She was beginning to feel like a traveller stranded at a busy station without a ticket to any place. Except she did, of course, have a return ticket from Charlotte to Heathrow.

★ ★ ★

'Dance?' Hiram Junior leaned forward across the table.

'I couldn't just yet. I ate too much, but it was a wonderful meal. Arnold was right about Creole food — those spicy crab cakes . . . '

'Nothing but the best. Shall we take coffee out in the courtyard? Brandy?'

'I've had enough, thanks.' She thought Hiram had, too, but she'd enjoyed his company. He'd made her laugh and flattered her outrageously. It was impossible not to enjoy being with the tall, attractive American. He danced wonderfully, too. The restaurant was filled with glamourous, expensively-dressed people. She stored it all up to tell Fiona when she got back to Stonebridge.

Outside, the summer night air was balmy — a huge, white, Carolina moon rode high over the trees, a splashing fountain and music from inside the restaurant made a soporific rhythm. A waiter brought coffee and brandy. There were only a few couples left at the discreetly-placed tables.

Hiram drained his brandy, then stood

up and took her hand.

'Let's walk. There's a stream down those steps. We'll come back to coffee.'

Before they reached the water Hiram drew her to a bench-seat under a tree.

'I can't wait much longer. Dang it. Lucy, you're making me real nervous. You'd never believe I've done this twice before. I'm just crazy for you.' He put his arms around her. 'You just gotta marry me. The moment I saw you at the airport, I knew. It has to be right this time. Dad's put a veto on us marrying again, but I'm thirty-four, and he's obviously crazy about you, too. He'll . . . '

'Hiram, please. I'm flattered and . . . ' She tried to think how to temper her refusal. 'I really like you. I've had a great evening, but I can't marry you.'

'Why not? Give me one good reason, and it'd better be good.'

'I don't love you. I'm sorry, but I don't . . . it wouldn't be fair.'

'What's that got to do with it? Did you love that Pete guy?'

'I thought I did.'

'But you don't now?'

'No. No, I don't.'

'So! You think you don't love me, but how do you know that?'

'I just do. Hiram, it's no good. You can't just make these things happen. I'm terrifically grateful to you — all the family, but . . . '

'I don't want your damned gratitude. I want you.' He crushed her against him, seeking her mouth, caught her lips for a second before she broke away.

'Don't, Hiram, please. I want us to stay friends. Don't make it hard. I'd like to fall in love with you, but it's not possible.'

He held her, still breathing hard, then moved away.

'OK. Maybe I've rushed you. Never was one for brilliant timing — but the Bojangles are a stubborn crew. I'm the oldest and so the most stubborn. I'm not giving you up. There's no one else back in England, is there?'

'No. There was only Pete.'

'And he's married now with a kid?'

'So I'm told.'

Lucy would have liked to go back to Palmetto but Hiram wanted to finish coffee and dance some more. He behaved so impeccably that by the end of the evening she wondered if she'd dreamt the scene by the tree.

But Hiram's fire for Lucy was smouldering deep. He'd fallen more and more in love with her, and her refusal had only tantalised him. He was an attractive and eligible young man and wasn't used to denial — this one was a challenge he couldn't bear to lose. He replanned his strategy.

To his annoyance, Daniel was at Palmetto when they got back.

'My God, Dan, how's the hospital coping without you. Hope you're bleep's working. Have a nightcap with us?'

'No thanks, it's late.'

'Not too late for Lucy and me. Our evening's just beginning.'

As she shrugged off her jacket, Hiram

came behind her to take it, his hands lingering on her shoulders as he brushed her neck with his lips. She tried to move away, conscious of Dan's eyes on her — cold and aloof.

Daniel's interruption was steel.

'I came to tell Dad I'm going to New York tonight. They're operating on Toby. There's pressure building up on his brain. It doesn't look good.'

'Oh, Dan, I'm so sorry. Is there anything I can do at all?' She broke away from Hiram's restraining hands.

'Nothing. There's no call to spoil the rest of your evening together.'

'Dan, it's not like . . . ' But the door had already slammed behind him. A couple of minutes later, Lucy heard his car roar off down the drive. Suddenly Palmetto Plantation seemed a vast and lonely place — a place she had no right to be . . .

Rain rattled the window and a loose screen tapped and flapped in the wind. Startled out of sleep, Lucy groped her way across the room. She snapped the catch and went back to bed. She'd pleaded tiredness to Hiram and escaped to her room after Dan had gone but it was ages before she'd fallen asleep. Looked like ages before she'd be back there, too.

The screen was still tapping — perhaps the catch was broken. She threw off the sheets, then stopped. It wasn't the screen, it was a different sound of tapping. Someone was tapping softly at her door. She looked at her watch. It was half past three! Pulling on a dressing-gown she crept to the door. The tapping intensified.

'Who . . . who is it?'

'Lucy, let me in — it's Hiram. I've got to talk to you.'

'Hiram, can't it wait till morning?'

'Let me in, Lucy.' His voice was loud.

She flipped the light switches so the room was brightly lit.

'The door's not locked.'

He stepped inside, closed the door and leaned against it.

'It's no good. I can't just leave it.

You've got to give me a chance.'

'A chance? I told you Hiram, I don't love you.'

'You will, in time. I'm determined, Lucy.' He took a step towards her. 'I mean business.' Before she could move away he'd caught her arm and pulled her to him. 'Don't fight it. Remember I kissed you on that first night — you didn't fight then?'

Lucy managed to pull away and, as calmly as possible, she said, 'Hiram, this is a mistake you'll regret in the morning. Why don't you go to bed now and we'll talk tomorrow? I'm really tired, and you must be exhausted. Please.' He seemed dazed, swaying a little on his feet. She fancied he'd been drinking and, with any luck, perhaps in the morning wouldn't remember coming to her room. Gently, she took his arm, opened the door and propelled him outside.

'Goodnight, Hiram. Get some sleep.' Quietly she closed the door, turned the key and slid the bolt across.

That settled it — she had to leave Palmetto, next day if possible, and certainly within the next forty-eight hours. She couldn't handle Hiram Junior, especially with Lisa gone — and now Dan. Dan! Her legs gave way and she dropped on the bed.

She certainly wasn't in love with Hiram, she knew that. What she blindly and stupidly hadn't realised before was that she was in love with Daniel Bojangle! She groaned and put her head under the pillows.

What a mess! What a terrible mess! And it was all her own fault. She should never have come, never got herself involved with the Bojangles in the first place. The only remedy was to remove herself from them as fast as she could.

Rain and strong winds buffeted Palmetto next morning. Hurricane Albert, the first hurricane of the season, whirled and grumbled in the Atlantic gathering force before deciding which part of the American coast to target.

Hiram Bojangle Junior summoned

his two brothers to an urgent meeting in the pool room.

'Just had a call from my mole, Henry. The situation is not as bad as we thought but it does prove the old man's going a bit crazy. He hasn't exactly left us destitute but our inheritance is hedged about with all sorts of penalties if we marry again, except,' he took a deep breath, 'hang on to your hats, boy — the bulk of the Bojangle empire goes to who — get this, marries Lucy Beaujangle.'

'Damn it, he is mad!' Scott exclaimed.

'My god, I don't believe it.' Corey's tan paled. 'Is it on the level? No kidding?'

'No kidding, and I promised Henry we'd keep it quiet, too — more than his professional life's worth if it got out. We've got to keep this under wraps.'

'What are we going to do?' Scott was the first to speak.

'I should maybe tell you, I asked Lucy to marry me last night.' Hiram looked a little sheepish.

159

'You . . . you . . . jumped the gun!'

'Calm down now, Corey. I'd no idea about all this. I just fell in love with her, that's all.'

'What did she say?'

'Needs time to think about it.'

There was an uneasy silence, each man pursuing his own thoughts.

'What we should do here is act as a team,' Scott said. 'OK, so Hiram's in there, but that don't preclude either of us. And I think we need some legal advice. How water tight is a provision like that? If we could prove Dad's not in full possession of his faculties, get a shrink in tow, especially while Dan's out of the way.'

'OK, let's sit on it for a day — meet again tomorrow. There is one thing though.' Hiram paused. 'Lucy Beaujangle can't be allowed to go back to the UK. Not yet, not until we decide what's best to be done. We gotta keep her here at Palmetto.'

★ ★ ★

Lucy woke late next morning, much to her annoyance. She'd set the alarm early but had slept through it. It was imperative she leave — that day if possible. She phoned the airport from her room. No flight from Charlotte was available that day or the next, although there was the possibility of cancellations the following day. The girl on the desk suggested flying from Atlanta and promised to phone back if she could secure a flight. It was the best she could do.

Waiting for the return call, Lucy began to pack. She'd have loved a swim but rain was lashing into the pool and low clouds scudded across the sky.

The phone rang. There was a flight from Atlanta to Gatwick the following day at noon. Lucy booked it provisionally to confirm later — when she'd worked out how to get to Atlanta!

The next immediate problem was Hiram Senior. The house was strangely silent as she went up to the top-floor suite. There was no one in the corridor or lifts. Palmetto had the air of the Marie Celeste. It was unnerving.

Nurse Paula greeted her suspiciously. Mr Hiram had not been too well in the night — must Lucy see him now?

'I must. I'm leaving tomorrow.'

'Tomorrow? But I thought . . . ' Paula stopped.

Corey had told her to keep an especially watchful eye on things in the sick room and report back any conversations between Lucy and his father.

'Paula, if that's Lucy, tell her to come in right now,' Hiram Senior called.

He was propped up in bed against a vast array of cushions.

'Lucy, come in. I've been waiting for you. I want to hear all about your date with Hiram last night. He give you a good time?'

'Yes. We had a lovely dinner. The Flamingo's a great place.'

'And you're going out with him again?'

'No. Hiram, I can't. I told you, I have to go home. I've booked a flight for

162

tomorrow from Atlanta. I hope . . . '
She broke off as Hiram gave a strangled
cry and slumped sideways.

'No. No!' He clawed the air. 'You
can't . . . shan't let you.' His breath
rasped in his throat as he fought to
speak, colour draining from his face.

Paula rushed into the room.

'Mr Hiram!' Paula glared at Lucy as
she rushed in. 'What've you done?
Quick, ring this number. He needs the
doctor, and it's all your fault.'

The doctor came almost immediately, followed by a team of consultants
and therapists. Consensus was that
Hiram had not had another stroke but
his blood pressure was sky high and he
needed absolute rest. Home nursing
could continue, as Hiram hated hospi-
tals, but he must remain quiet. No
visitors were allowed except immediate
family.

From then on there was a subtle
difference in the household's attitude to
Lucy. Nurse Paula let it be known it
was Lucy's fault, by announcing her

departure so abruptly — and after everyone had been so kind to her, too. From being the petted, honoured guest from England, she was suddenly bad news. The ungrateful visitor from the UK acquired outcast status.

She also found it impossible to leave the house. Once she knew Hiram would recover she finished packing and confirmed her flight from Atlanta. The problem was, she couldn't get to Atlanta!

The Bojangle sons had visited their father, then disappeared for the day. Hiram had spoken to her briefly before leaving.

'You can't leave now, Lucy. It'd kill the old man.'

'But I've a flight booked tomorrow from Atlanta.'

'You must unbook it then. I'll be back tonight. We'll talk later.'

It was only when Lucy tried to make arrangements for transport to Atlanta the following day that she realised how isolated Palmetto could be. Strangely, no estate vehicle was available, and no one was free to drive her, even into Charleston, let alone Atlanta.

'Best wait until Mr Hiram Junior, or Mr Scott or Mr Corey come back,'was all the help she could get.

By the end of the day she knew there was a tacit conspiracy to keep her at Palmetto. She was forced to cancel her Atlanta flight and wait, a virtual prisoner, albeit in the most comfortable and luxurious of prisons.

9

Lucy felt increasingly isolated. She'd hoped for help from one of the many visitors and friends usually in and out at Palmetto, but no one came near. Maybe the spell of rough weather kept people away, but she suspected a more sinister motive.

Hiram Junior knew he must rein in his growing obsession for Lucy, and tread warily. It was a new experience for him to be thwarted and he wasn't sure how to play it. The brothers, too, were edgy with each other. Hiram Senior's eccentricity and paranoia were proving breeding grounds for greed and suspicion.

Lucy took refuge swimming whenever she could, even braving the rain storms. It was warm rain anyway and the pool was sheltered from the high winds. On the third day after Hiram

Senior's 'collapse' Lucy climbed out of the water and saw a tall figure on the diving board at the other end.

'Dan,' she called, and ran towards him. 'Thank goodness you've come home!'

She couldn't help it, sheer relief that help had finally arrived overwhelmed her. She flung herself into his arms, and a wave of intense feeling ran through her.

'Hey, hey, what's the matter?'

'I'm so glad to see you.' She put her head against his chest.

'Something has happened, hasn't it?' He cupped her head and tilted it back to look at her, her body soft and warmly damp pressing against him. He bent his head and kissed her and nothing on earth could stop Lucy's body responding.

She put her arms round his neck and kissed him back. He felt so safe, so strong. When he finally released her, his eyes were dark, but not the dangerous dark she'd glimpsed in Hiram's eyes, a softer yet more intense passion.

'Lucy,' he murmured, and kissed her again.

She tore herself away.

'Dan, I forgot, how dreadful! How's Toby? And Lisa, and Arnold's family. What must you think of me?'

'I think . . . I think I must kiss you again. Toby's making progress. The operation was a success, but they still can't be certain of the damage. The worst scenario is that he might be paralysed from the waist down. The best is that he'll walk out the hospital and marry Lisa next year. Arnold and Joelle will be in New York for a while longer. Lisa's coming back next week. Now tell me what's happened here. I know Dad's not well but . . . '

'I want to go back to England. I booked a flight but no one would take me to Atlanta. I know it sounds crazy but I feel like a prisoner, and Hiram . . . '

'And Hiram what?' His eyes narrowed.

'They all blame me for your father's collapse. I told him I'd booked a flight.'

'Must you go then?' His voice was filled with concern.

'Yes, I must. I need to go home to . . . to start my life again.'

The urgent shrilling of his bleeper interrupted them.

'Damn!' Dan let her go. 'I thought it was a mite too quiet. I'll take you to any airport you like.' He punched a number on his mobile phone. 'Just so long as you promise . . . ' His face changed dramatically as he listened to the voice on the phone. 'When? How long? Both of them? I'll be there.' He was pulling on clothes, rubbing his rain-soaked body perfunctorily. 'Hospital. Emergency, and it's Megan and Chloe. If anything happens I'll never . . . I might be gone a while . . . '

'But what . . . ?'

'No time. Just pray.'

Grabbing jacket and tie he ran across the terrace as though chased by devils.

Now what? Lucy wrapped a towel

round her and sat under cover, staring out at the rain. Megan and Chloe — obviously that's where his heart was! She made up her mind there and then — no point hanging about. The best person to rely on was herself. She'd simply walk out. The main road was only a few miles away. She'd hitch a ride to the nearest town and hire a car, stay in Charlotte or Atlanta, whichever direction the ride took her, and wait for the first available flight out.

Why on earth hadn't she done that before? She knew why — subconsciously she'd been waiting for Dan. Well, she'd seen him. No point waiting any longer.

The action plan lifted her spirits. She jettisoned her luggage down to one small bag, wrote a note to Hiram Senior, and took one last look at her luxurious suite. The cottage would look pretty cramped by comparison, but at least it was home. Her own home!

The house was still quiet. She knew Hiram Junior and Corey were out at

170

meetings. Scott was nowhere to be seen. Lucy didn't intend creeping out like a thief but she was glad not to meet anyone, though it saddened her to think of the contrast between arrival and departure.

The rain increased in ferocity, flooding down in grey sheets, but at least no one was about. She set off down the long drive, the Spanish mossed oaks giving some protection from the storm warnings of Hurricane Albert.

★　★　★

'What d'you mean, she's gone? You were supposed to keep a look out.' Hiram Junior accused Scott. 'Where's she gone?'

'I dunno. She was in the pool this morning, spite of the rain. I saw Dan with her — getting along fine, too. I'd say he's ahead of you, Hiram.'

'You leave Daniel to me. I can soon sort that out. I want her back, and I'm going to marry her. You've got to help me.'

'Help you to our inheritance? What kind of fools do you take us for?' Corey joined in.

'Look, we decided, whoever does marry Lucy, not that it's going to be either of you, signs a legal document sharing the estate equally as Dad originally intended. Otherwise we lose the lot, to be administered by a charitable trust! Ugh! We'd be at the mercy of Dad's financial wizards. No, marrying Lucy Beaujangle's the only way, and pretty fast, too, before the old man dies!'

'Come on, Hiram, you can't make the girl marry you. This is America — we don't have forced marriages.'

Scott was beginning to feel Hiram was going over the top on this. There was a fanatical gleam in his eyes which was a mite unnerving. Scott had seen that same gleam when Hiram was playing tennis. He had to win whatever the cost.

'Let her go. We'll fight the damned will in court if needs be.'

'And pay mega bucks to the lawyers to hang it out for years? No fear, and I want Lucy Beaujangle, inheritance or no, and she wants me, too — just isn't ready to accept it yet. Still hung up over this Pete guy back in England.'

Corey spoke decisively.

'Hiram's right. Once he's married Lucy we have to trust him to do right by us, so let's work this out together. She can't have gone far on foot, and there are only two roads out of here. Hiram and I'll go. Scott, you stay here in case she comes back. Calm her down and keep her here.'

Outside, mercifully, the rain had stopped but Lucy was already soaked. Her case grew heavier by the minute and the few vehicles that did pass threw up muddy spray and showed no inclination to stop. Once out of Palmetto gates she'd taken an unmetalled dirt road but she wasn't sure where it led.

Ten minutes on, the lights of a vehicle bobbed in the distance and the rain started again. She turned to face the oncoming car and put out a hopeful thumb. Thank goodness — it was stopping. She picked up her case as the door opened.

'Can you give me a . . . '

'Get in, Lucy. What on earth are you doing out here?'

'Hiram!' She backed away but he reached out and grabbed her arm.

'Don't be stupid. You won't be able to make it to the main highway. I'm taking you back to Palmetto.' He looked reproachfully at her. 'Why're you running away from us? Don't you know we all love you, and make up your mind to it — you're going to marry me.'

A huge clap of thunder decided her. No time for heroics, her attempt had failed. 'All right. I don't have much choice do I?'

'Not a deal — and there are worse fates.'

Thankfully, she got into the car and leaned back against the cushioned upholstery. It was so nice to be inside!

'Sorry, I'm making the car pretty wet.'

'It'll dry out. Soon have you in a hot bath and into dry clothes. You are a little fool. What're you scared of, running off like that?'

'I just felt . . . trapped. You, no one would take me to the airport. I didn't realise it would be so difficult.'

'We're all real concerned about you. It hurts you couldn't trust us, Lucy.'

'I'm sorry. Maybe I was wrong, I don't know. I just felt . . . '

Hiram was being so nice it was difficult not to feel ashamed of herself. Perhaps she had been over-hasty — paranoid about being kept at Palmetto.

Hiram spun the wheel suddenly to avoid one of the many pot-holes.

'Here's a deal,' he said.

'A deal?' The Bojangles were deal mad!

'Yeah. You know Dad's set on you marrying into the family?'

'What!'

'Yeah. Seems to think it's the only way to counter what he calls our predatory bimbos — ex-wives, he means. Don't ask me. He's not as clear-headed as he used to be. You know he's pretty sick, too?'

'Yes, but . . . '

'Hear me out. The doctors say he hasn't got long to live, so how about you and I giving him what he wants? He'd die happy, Lucy, if you and I were to marry.'

'Hiram, we've been through all this before. I don't love you. I can't marry just to please your father. He wouldn't want us to marry without love.'

'Sometimes the most successful marriages are arranged. Any case, I've got enough love for the both of us.'

'Maybe but I can't . . . '

'If you're thinking of brother Daniel,' Hiram said harshly, 'forget it. He's set to marry one of his social disaster clients. Some woman with a kid already. Set her up in one of his housing projects.'

'Dan — marrying Megan!' A wave of intense misery swept through her.

'You know her?' Hiram asked.

'I met her when Dan . . . he took me to see . . .'

'Well, then, you'll know.'

Yes, she did know, had known all along.

'I still can't marry you,' she said dully. 'It makes no difference what Daniel does.' Although it did — nothing mattered more.

'I'm a patient guy, and maybe I've rushed things a bit. You'll come round to it soon, I know you will, but OK, I'll back off for now — if you agree to a deal.'

'What deal?'

'To please the old man, we'll have a mock marriage ceremony. Let him think we're married . . .'

'You're getting crazier by the minute, Hiram. I couldn't possibly do that. How could you think of deceiving your father like that?' But as she spoke, Lucy knew she didn't care, didn't care any more what happened to her. Pete had deceived her, so had Dan, kissing her as though it meant something.

Even her father — he'd deceived his family, pretending everything was all right when it patently wasn't. What did one more deception matter?

'Just suppose . . . just suppose I did agree, what'd happen then, afterwards?'

'Afterwards, I'd fly you to Charlotte, put you on a plane to London, tell Dad you'd gone to sort out your affairs . . . '

'He wouldn't be fooled.'

'Lucy, we have to face it — Dad isn't going to last that long.'

'It seems so awful. And what about the rest of the family? It's a lunatic idea.'

'They'll go along with it for Dad's sake.'

'You promise I can go home, no strings attached?'

'No strings. I can't promise not to follow you to England.'

'No deal then.'

'OK. Only if you say so.'

Hiram believed in the present, the

future he could manipulate. Triumph surged through him. He'd got this far, and he was going to win.

'We'll do it tonight, before it's too late.'

'Tonight! How? Can't we just tell your father, tell him we're going to be married?' She hated saying it. Deceit was alien — she couldn't go through with it. 'Hiram, I . . . '

'Just leave everything to me. Dry out, rest up and get Sue to lay out your best outfit. It'll take me an hour or so to set things in motion.'

'What things?'

'Nothing for you to worry about, everything'll be fine. You're doing the right thing. Think of Dad, how happy it'll make him.'

He took Lucy up to the guest suite and kissed her lightly on the cheek.

'I promise, Lucy, no strings. A few words by an actor pal of mine in Dad's room and he'll die a happy man. I'll get Corey and Scott in to make it look authentic. Have a good rest now. I'll send Sue in to give you a hand.'

'I don't need a hand, thanks. And I'm still not sure . . . '

'Trust me,' he said, 'I'll call back for you when I've fixed it.'

Outside, Hiram Junior punched the air with his fist in victory, then went to make some phone calls and find his two brothers, praying that Dan would follow his usual pattern and keep well away from Palmetto for the rest of the day.

Sue knocked on Lucy's door, waited a few seconds then went in.

'Miss Lucy, Mr Hiram says are you ready and here's some champagne to put you in the mood, whatever that means.'

Lucy was sitting at the vanity unit brushing her hair.

'Come in, Sue. Thanks. Where is he?'

'In Mr Hiram Senior's room. The old gentleman's perked up by all accounts. Something Mr Hiram told him.'

Well, I'm sorry, Lucy thought. I'll be the villainess again, but I'm not doing it. It had been ridiculous even to contemplate it. She'd go along and tell both Hirams it was all a mistake, and tomorrow she'd phone a car-hire firm and drive herself to Charlotte.

Champagne bubbled in the glass on the table. She picked it up and drank thirstily. Dutch courage coursed through her veins — that's what she needed. It'd be easy to tell them how ludicrous it was. She poured another glass.

'Right, I'll go and join him.' She set the empty glass on the table.

It was like a scene from a movie. The old man sat in his wheelchair by the bed, dressed in a tuxedo; Hiram Junior on his right hand, Scott and Corey behind the chair — all three in white tuxedos. Both Hirams had red carnations in their buttonholes. Lucy saw flowers everywhere, white and pink roses, carnations, giving off a heavy scent. There was another man with a book, some papers on a table.

'Lucy!' Hiram Senior put his hand

out to her. 'You have made me the happiest man tonight. Here — a wedding present, the first of many.' He gave her a long, leather box. 'Open it later, when you and Hiram are alone.'

Lucy tried to move, to say something, but she couldn't. She heard the words in her head, 'No, no, I can't,' but nothing came out. Her legs were like lead.

Hiram Junior stepped forward, took her arm, then held her firmly round the waist.

'I . . . ' she croaked.

'Guess she's mighty nervous.' Hiram motioned Corey to come to her other side. 'Take her arm,' he hissed as the other man began to speak.

'Stop!' she heard in her head. She felt awful. The room began to spin, but she was firmly held by the two brothers.

Voices came from all over the room to congratulate her, and tell her about the honeymoon. Then waves of nausea spun her into blackness. It was the last thing she remembered for a while.

Light streamed into the unfamiliar room — a huge bedroom. She lifted her head and dropped it back quickly. It hurt! Her mouth was dry. Where on earth . . . ? She tried to remember. The picture window looked out over hills — or mountains — it was difficult to tell, they were so shrouded by rain.

Tree tops were bent by gale-force winds. Even in the quiet, double-glazed room she could hear the crashing and roaring outside. There was a great log fire in the open fireplace. Where was she? Had she been in an accident? She struggled to sit up, winced at the pain. There was a carafe of water by the bedside. She poured a glass and sipped it thankfully. The door opened.

'Good morning, Lucy. Feeling better — Mrs Bojangle? Ready to start married life? I've brought you breakfast in bed.'

'Where . . . where are we?'

Hiram Junior put down the tray and

went over to the window.

'North Carolina, the Blue Ridge Mountains. The family mountain cabin where we come for peace and quiet — and honeymoons! Blowing Rock's the nearest town, ten miles away.

'The weather's going to be rough for a couple of days — Hurricane Albert's about to sweep through. It should be pretty spectacular. We won't be able to get out, but then we won't want to, will we? There's just the two of us. Pretty idyllic start, uh?'

He came over to the bed.

10

Hiram! What do you think you're doing? I don't want you to come any nearer. You're mad!'

'Aw, honey, I'm not going to hurt you. I love you!'

'I've told you over and over, I don't love you. I can't possibly marry you.'

'Too late, and you know it.' He laughed. 'Willing enough yesterday in Dad's suite. Preacher joined us for life, and I'm going to make it stick for just that — life! Dad was real cockahoop, too.'

'But you told me he was an actor. And you kidnapped me — I'm not staying.'

'Take a look outside. No one but a fool'd go out in those forests in a hurricane.'

'I heard someone last night.' She clutched desperately at straws.

'That was Lou and Jim. They take care of the place. I sent them away. They've a small place down the mountain. Now eat your breakfast and I'll show you around.' He put the tray on her bed.

Lucy poured coffee and tried to stop her hands from shaking.

'You surely don't want to keep me here against my will?'

'I shan't force you. You'll come to me of your own free will — because you love me. For some reason you aren't admitting it yet but you will, and pretty soon.'

He sat on the edge of the bed, touched her hair and ran his finger down her cheek.

'Admit it,' he said softly, 'just say you love me. I knew you did that first night when you kissed me . . . '

'I kissed you!' Lucy was appalled. 'That was just friendly . . . I'd just arrived and you were so kind and welcoming on the plane. I was grateful.'

'You could've fooled me. Wise up,

Lucy. I attract you, and now I'm megarich, or will be when Dad dies, especially now . . . '

'I don't care about money!'

'You will, when I tell you Dad's left most of the Bojangle empire to whoever marries Lucy Beaujangle. How about that?'

For a second she couldn't speak, then as the full impact hit, she pushed him back violently, upsetting the breakfast trays, scattering crockery and cutlery.

'You . . . you . . . monster! How could you?' She leaped out of bed. 'Where've you put my clothes? I'm getting out of here, hurricane or no.' Grabbing a bed cover she wrapped it round her near-naked figure. 'My clothes,' she hissed.

'What's wrong, Lucy? I reckon you should be pleased. See how much we all think of you. Dad's mad keen to get you into the family.'

'Mad is spot on. You're all mad. Oh, what's the use! We live on different planets and I'm leaving this one. Right now.'

'I had Sue pack a bag for you. It's through in the bathroom, but you're not going anywhere. You're my wife.'

He made a grab for her but she eluded him, reached the bathroom and slammed the door.

'Lucy!' Hiram banged his fists against the wood. 'Don't be so damned difficult. OK, take your time to cool off. I'll check the fuel store. We'll talk later.'

'Not if I can help it,' Lucy muttered angrily.

Thank goodness Sue had had the sense to pack waterproofs and boots, obviously anticipating rough, mountain weather. She listened by the door. Had he gone to check the fuel or was he outside waiting to pounce?

With a terrible sense of déja vu she unlocked the door. The bedroom was deserted. Outside, a wide gallery led to an open-tread staircase. She tiptoed down the steps. A distant thumping indicated Hiram may indeed be stacking wood. Zipping up her waterproof she ran to the door and was outside in a flash.

The wind took her breath as it tried to hurl her back against the side of the house, but she fought back and battled towards a dirt track heading away from the building and down the mountainside.

The Bojangle house was high up the wooded slopes, with no other dwelling above it as far as she could see. The wind was behind now, pushing her headlong down the track so fast she could barely keep her feet. Then she saw it! Far down and still some way off, just visible through the trees, the solid square stone of a neighbouring chimney stack.

She turned to gauge how far she'd run and saw Hiram pounding down on her. She looked at the chimney and knew she couldn't outrun him. She hesitated a fraction and made a decision.

Arms outstretched, she ran backwards towards him.

'Hiram, thank goodness — I'm so

scared. The wind just blew me down. I was trying to get back. I came out to see . . . '

'You fool.' He reached her and clutched her arm. 'It's dangerous out here. See those trees?' he yelled above the howling gale. 'Any minute one could come down.' Half carrying, half lifting, he dragged her back to the house. Once inside he collapsed against the door and let her go.

'I'm sorry, I didn't understand. I just thought I'd go a little way to see.' She smiled at him. 'I promise I won't go out again.'

He put his hands on her shoulders, looked intently into her eyes.

'Seeing sense at last! Knew you would, given time, and we've a lifetime of that.' He put his arms round her. 'Now you rest, have a hot tub — and there's a sauna in the basement. I'm going to cook us a real special meal.'

'That'd be nice. I'd like to try the sauna — perhaps a nap. I still feel the effects of that champagne. It really knocked me out.'

'Good girl.'

He kissed her, his eyes dark, and Lucy's stomach turned as he left the room.

He spent the rest of the day in the kitchen, cooking. It was getting dark when she joined him for dinner.

'Smells good. Where'd you learn to cook?' It was an effort to keep her voice light and even.

'Mom saw to it that all us boys could fend for ourselves. I kinda took to it.' He threw chicken pieces into sizzling oil, 'Dan, too — we used to have cook-out barbecue competitions until it got so serious Mom put a stop to it.'

'Like the tennis tournament?'

'Guess so. This is nearly done. Can you check on the dining table? Stuff's all out there in the cupboards. Make it real fancy. Our first night together!'

He put his hands on her waist and she sensed his passion.

'Hiram, the chicken. It's burning.

Special, you said,' she beguiled, guessing his intention to let supper go hang.

'OK, you win. For the moment!'

He turned his attention back to the cooker and Lucy let out her breath in relief.

'I'll go and fix the table then.'

This would definitely be her last chance. By the front door she kicked off her house shoes and pulled on boots and waterproofs she'd concealed earlier. It'd have to be third time lucky. Outside, it was about dark enough to hide her, but light enough to show up the dirt track — and she was running on it for her life.

She ran on, not daring to look back, anxiously peering ahead for a glimpse of the friendly chimney. Nothing! An aching stitch in her side slowed her down, and there it was, almost in hailing distance, a dark, squat shape. But there were no lights, and the place had a deserted, closed-down look.

Fearful, she glanced up as the wind mocked and howled, bending the trees almost horizontal. She retreated to the comparative shelter of the porch and contemplated her options, finding the prospect dismal. She shivered, keeping an eye on the swaying branches above.

Then she heard the sound she dreaded — an engine in the distance. Hiram was coming after her! Pressed against the porch she waited for the sweeping headlights to pinpoint her hiding place — but there was something odd!

The lights were coming from the wrong direction — up the mountain track not down it from the Bojangle cabin. A slim chance of help — it had to be! Shielding her eyes from the oncoming dazzle, she ran out towards the headlights, waving for the truck to stop.

It was coming too fast! Had the driver seen her? She jumped away as the vehicle skidded to a halt and the lights dimmed. In that same moment a curious pain settled in her heart as she saw the driver. Dan!

He opened the door, calling out to her. At the same time she heard a groaning roar, looked up, and saw a tree tilt and start a deadly, slow-motion descent.

'Lucy — run. Back!' She saw Dan leap away before the almighty crash which shook the earth where she'd been standing. Where the vehicle had been, there was nothing but a mass of branches sprouting awkwardly from the fallen trunk.

Lucy lunged forward pulling aside boughs, desperately searching for the vehicle, dreading she'd find a tangled wreck with Dan inside. The fallen tree mocked her puny efforts. Her hands were torn and bleeding yet she couldn't stop scrabbling at the jagged wood.

'Lucy?' the voice, sharp and disembodied, floated above her.

'Dan! Where are you?'

'Here.' Balanced precariously on a branch he slithered along the trunk, swung out and landed lightly beside her.

'You're safe! Dan, I was so afraid!' She wanted to throw her arms around him, but in the stormy darkness he was distant and remote.

'The vehicle's smashed. Just managed to jump clear.' He hunched his shoulders against the wind, 'The road's blocked. What in the world are you doing here? Don't you know it's dangerous to be out in a hurricane?'

'I do now. Hiram said . . . '

'So, the two of you are at the cabin!' His interruption was brusque.

'Yes, but I need to . . . '

'I'll take you back to him.'

'No!' She pulled him back. 'I . . . can't. I ran away.'

'Scott told me you were married last night. Where were you running to?'

'I saw a house down the mountain — the couple who look after your house?'

'Jim and Lou. They're probably down in the valley with their daughter. It's safer. Lucy.' He swung her round to

195

face him. 'Are you married to Hiram?'

'He says I am. I don't remember much about it. He asked me to pretend to marry him, to please your father. But I couldn't do it. Then he sent champagne, and I'm sure now there was something in it. I felt drugged . . . I just don't know. I remember a man, and your dad and brothers all dressed up.' She shook her head in misery. 'It's . . . it's like some horrible nightmare.'

'Come on, back to the cabin.' He touched her shoulder. 'It's time to straighten out a few things with my brother.'

Lucy had a hard time keeping up with Dan's long strides, but as they neared the lights of the cabin he waited for her.

'You go in. I'm right behind you.'

'Must I?' She hung back. 'I'm scared. I've run away twice, no, three times. You never came back to Palmetto,' she accused, remembering his promise, and his kiss by the pool.

'Go,' he repeated. 'I'm here now.'

Hiram was seated in a chair facing the front door, a half-empty bottle by his feet. His face was dark with anger but she said firmly, 'I tried to run away again. It was silly. I was frightened of you, but I know you'll help me . . . '

'I'll help you,' he interrupted. 'You're my wife — Mrs Hiram Bojangle IV, and I'm going to make damn sure you are just that.' He got up instantly and moved swiftly enough to grab her and push her against the wall. 'Don't you ever dare run out on me again.' His mouth came down punishingly on hers.

She twisted and tried to fight him off but he was too strong. She raised her fists but he caught both her hands and held them down. Pinned and powerless, she threw her head back.

'Hiram, don't.'

Suddenly his body was plucked away and hurled across the room to crash on to a sofa. Dan strode over and picked him up by his shirt.

'What the devil are you playing at? You never learn, do you? You can't simply take what you want like a spoiled kid. You can't force yourself on Lucy.'

He gave him a shake but Hiram wrenched free and spat back, 'I'm not forcing her, she wants me . . . we're married — and there's nothing you can do about it. You want her yourself! You don't like losing! You've always wanted what I had, but this time I've beaten you. I've got the girl, I've got the money, so you can clear off back to your little hippy in the woods.'

'Don't,' Lucy screamed as Dan raised his fist. 'You'll kill him.'

'I'd like to.' He dropped his arm. 'But he's too drunk to hit back.' He pushed his brother back on the sofa. 'I'm going and Lucy's coming with me.'

'You lay a finger and I'll sue you for alienation . . . assault . . . ' Hiram's words were slurred. He staggered across the room to Lucy. 'Tell him, tell him you're staying with me. Goddammit, it's our honeymoon. Tell him you love me.'

Then Lucy felt nothing but pity for him. She knew what it was like to love and not be loved in return. Hiram was like a madman, a changed character from the guy who'd met her at the airport. She had to convince him she didn't love him.

'Hiram, I never loved you. I couldn't . . . because I'm in love with someone else. I'm sorry, I should have told you before.' The silence seemed to last for ever. Behind her, Daniel was very still. 'I'm sorry,' she repeated, 'but you do see — I have to leave, married or not.'

'If you were forced into the ceremony it'll have no legal standing,' Dan said.

Hiram slumped back on the sofa, head in his hands. No one spoke until he finally looked at Lucy.

'Guess I've been a fool. I really fell for you — and that was before Dad changed his will. I expect Scott told you about that,' he said to Dan, 'and that we were here.'

'Yes, he did. He was kinda jumpy about the whole thing, but Arnold'll rip the codicil to pieces in court. But if we all act together we can persuade Dad to change his mind. You're a damned idiot, Hiram. Always were. You just can't stop playing games — only this time you've gone 'way over.'

Hiram shrugged in defeat.

'May as well tell you the rest. What Scott didn't tell you, because no one else knew, is that the whole thing was a fake. An actor friend of mine was the preacher. I thought once I'd got Lucy up here, on my own . . . don't worry.' He saw the horror in her face. 'I intended making an honest woman of you. That charade at Palmetto was to please the old man. I thought he was pretty near the end.'

'Your wedding perked him up considerably.' Dan was grim. 'He'll still be around for quite a while to plague us with his games. You're as bad as one another. It's time to get tough with Dad, stop him playing God, and time you stopped your tricks and grew up!'

For a minute Lucy thought the

brothers would fight as they stood tense, eyeball to eyeball, then all at once Hiram relaxed.

'OK, you win this one.' He held out his hand and Dan shook it. 'Well, that's that then. Guess we could all use some coffee.'

'I'll make it.'

Lucy fled to the kitchen, thankful to be alone to still her knees, still trembling with tension. After they'd calmed down over a coffee, Dan rose to his feet.

'Time to go,' he said turning to Lucy, who breathed an inward sigh of relief.

'Are you sure he'll be all right?' she said as she turned in her car seat to look back at the disappearing cabin lights.

'Sure. Storm's blowing over, and Hiram needs some time to think. All his life he's had these . . . fixations. He gets kinda blinkered and obsessive. Same with all his wives. He and Dad, game-players both. Rescue crews'll have the main track clear by tomorrow.

Lucky for us Lisa left her little car at the cabin, and I know a way back out through the woods.'

He drove on in silence for a while, concentrating on what looked to Lucy like a mere bridle path through the trees.

'I'm sorry my family put you through all this.' Dan stared ahead. 'Arnold should never have brought you to Palmetto. He knows Dad — and Hiram!'

'It was my choice and, apart from just lately, it's been great.'

Dan's knuckles were taut on the wheel.

'There's the main track ahead — joins the highway to Charleston. Be back at Palmetto in about five hours.'

Lucy glanced at his stoney profile.

'Dan, could you . . . I don't want to go back to Palmetto. Could you take me to Charlotte . . . to the airport?'

'There'll be no planes out until tomorrow.'

'It doesn't matter. I can stay the night somewhere. A motel.'

'Pretty anxious to leave, get back to this lover of y . . . ' He stopped the car with a screech and turned to face her. 'Dang it, Lucy, just what game are you playing? You come over here, break up the Bojangle family, make us all fall in love with you — then you want out. Back to England — '

Lucy stared at him in amazement.

'What do you mean, Dan? Make us all fall in love?'

'I'll take you to the airport, throw you on the next plane, get away fast and try to forget you ever came near Palmetto.' He wrenched at the ignition key.

Lucy put her hand over his to stop him.

'You're going to marry Megan. Why should my leaving . . . ?'

'Megan! Marry Megan?'

'Hiram said so. And the three of you . . . you all looked so happy together . . . '

'Marry Megan. She's already married, poor girl — to a vicious brute who's tried to kill her more than once. She's been trying to hide from him. We thought she'd done it, but he found them at the new house and attacked them both. But for the site workers he'd have killed them.

'That's why I had to get to the hospital. It was touch and go for Megan but she'll be OK — and I had to arrange care for Chloe. When I got back to Palmetto and Scott told me you and Hiram were married, I was so mad I came after you. Of course I'm not in love with Megan.' He looked at her. 'Unfortunately, I'm in love with you, Lucy, and that's why I've gotta put you on that plane.'

'But why?' Lucy's heart was pounding its own tempestuous rhythm.

'Because, you idiot, I can't stand the idea of you and someone else. When you told Hiram you were in love with someone else, it's you I could have killed, not my brother. Kinda scary feeling. So back you go!'

'No. Please. Don't start the car for a

minute. I need to tell you ... the person I'm in love with ... it's ... it's you.'

In the dim interior of the small car she saw his eyes flash and then she was in his arms, and he was kissing her as she remembered he had — once before.

'Dan,' she said breathlessly, 'is it really true? You love me? You seemed so angry when I first came to Palmetto — as though you hated me.'

'I was as much a fool as Hiram. Guess I got the wires crossed. Thought you were some sort of gold-digger. Then I started to fall in love with you, and when Scott told me you and Hiram ... '

'Ssh.' She put a finger to his lips. 'I don't want to think about that.'

'You will marry me, Lucy?' He kissed her again.

'Yes ... oh, no ... of course I can't marry you.'

'Of course you will.'

'No. Don't you see — the money. Your father's will. It'll look like ... '

He stopped her with a kiss and said, 'Dad'll change that, but in any case, I bartered my inheritance years back in exchange for Dad's founding a new research unit for the hospital, among other things. So all you're getting is a working surgeon — not a millionaire.'

'Dan, as if I care about the money! I never felt life at Palmetto was for real. It's you I love.'

'Stop talking, Lucy. We've wasted enough time. Come here.'

She hadn't far to go! And she never wanted to leave the sweet comfort of Dan's arms ever again. Lucy Beaujangle knew she'd finally come home.

THE END

We do hope that you have enjoyed reading this large print book.

Did you know that all of our titles are available for purchase?

We publish a wide range of high quality large print books including:
Romances, Mysteries, Classics General Fiction Non Fiction and Westerns

Special interest titles available in large print are:
The Little Oxford Dictionary Music Book, Song Book Hymn Book, Service Book

Also available from us courtesy of Oxford University Press:
Young Readers' Dictionary (large print edition) Young Readers' Thesaurus (large print edition)

For further information or a free brochure, please contact us at:
**Ulverscroft Large Print Books Ltd., The Green, Bradgate Road, Anstey, Leicester, LE7 7FU, England.
Tel:** (00 44) **0116 236 4325
Fax:** (00 44) **0116 234 0205**

VISIONS OF THE HEART

Christine Briscomb

When property developer Connor Grant contracted Natalie Jensen to landscape the grounds of his large country house near Ashley in South Australia, she was ecstatic. But then she discovered he was acquiring — and ripping apart — great swathes of the town. Her own mother's house and the hall where the drama group met were two of his targets. Natalie was desperate to stop Connor's plans — but she also had to fight the powerful attraction flowing between them.

YESTERDAY'S LOVE

Stella Ross

Jessica's return from Africa to claim her inheritance of 'Simon's Cottage', and take up medicine in her home town, is the signal for her past to catch up with her. She had thought the short affair she'd had with her cousin Kirk twelve years ago a long-forgotten incident. But Kirk's unexpected return to England, on a last-hope mission to save his dying son, sparks off nostalgia. It leads Jessica to rethink her life and where it is leading.

FINGALA, MAID OF RATHAY

Mary Cummins

On his deathbed, Sir James Montgomery of Rathay asks his daughter, Fingala, to swear that she will not honour her marriage contract until her brother Patrick, the new heir, returns from serving the King. Patrick must marry. Rathay must not be left without a mistress. But Patrick has fallen in love with the Lady Catherine Gordon whom the King, James IV, has given in marriage to the young man who claims to be Richard of York, one of the princes in the Tower.